Joshua

A Novel
By Robert Fishell

A Boy at a Crossroads

Life is bleak for 12-year-old Joshua Miller. He's failing in school, his teachers pick on him, his classmates laugh at him, a relentless bully terrorizes him, his best friend has moved away, and he's hopelessly in love with the prettiest girl in his school.

At home, his harsh and distant father has all but disinherited him, he worries his mother to tears, and he squabbles senselessly with his pretty, talented sister Anica, who seems to be everything he is not. Then adolescence comes along and really complicates things.

A torrent of long-denied feelings for a sister who once adored him compel Joshua to repair the damage he's done to their relationship. His longtime babysitter helps him to understand things his mother doesn't know how to tell him and his father doesn't want him to know. Then, in a murky funeral home far away from home, he meets a distant cousin who changes his life in ways he could never have imagined.

As Joshua starts to turn his life around, his father's tortured past catches up with him, and life at home begins to unravel. Joshua is faced with a decision that could imperil his very life. He will risk everything to protect his sister, and in the process, he learns the power of love and the meaning of courage.

For George

Table of Contents

Acknowledgments

I could not have produced this book without the support of my family, who gave me the encouragement I needed to press on with a project that became much larger than I anticipated.

My sister Mary and her husband Jerry read through an earlier draft of this book and gave me some suggestions that proved valuable, helping me to shore up some parts of the book that clearly needed it.

Cover Photography:
Tatiana Bobkova/Shutterstock
NOAA

Being deeply loved by someone gives you strength. Loving someone deeply gives you courage. – Lao Tzu, 6th Century B.C.E.

Josh and Ani

"It's still your turn Ani. You got a double."

"I don't want to use the other one."

"You have to use it. It's a rule."

"I don't want to!"

"Why not?"

"Because I'll win."

"Why don't you want to win?"

"Because you'll be sad."

"No I won't! I wasn't sad the last game."

"But it's your turn to win!"

Joshua scratched his head for a moment.

"I don't think it works like that."

Anica swept her hand across the board, scattering the cards and the pieces.

"Then it's a dumb game! And there isn't even any candy!" Anica exclaimed. Tears welled in her pretty brown eyes.

Joshua swept his own hand across the board, scattering the cards and pieces farther.

"You know what, Ani? It is a dumb game!" Joshua made a silly face and picked up the box, dumping the rest of the tokens and the rule sheet onto the floor. With both hands, he started to scramble everything. Anica started to laugh and joined in. Soon, the brightly colored cards and the little plastic game pieces were everywhere. Joshua and his sister faced one another across the wreckage, now laughing together.

"What are you two doing?" Their mother exclaimed.

"Hi Mommy!" Anica said happily. "Can we have some ice cream?"

"Not until you and your brother clean up this mess, you can't!"

Joshua and Anica quickly gathered up everything and dumped it into the box. Joshua put the lid on it and shoved it under his bed.

"We're supposed to put it away."

"I'll do it later," Joshua proclaimed, knowing full well that he wouldn't. "C'mon Ani, let's get some ice cream!"

Joshua and Anica sat at the kitchen table savoring the cherry vanilla ice cream their mother had served them.

"Josh, do you have to go to school tomorrow?"

"Tomorrow's Thursday. I have to go to school on Thursdays."

"What's first grade like?"

"It's dumb. The teacher yells at me."

Anica pouted. She was mad. Mommy was already scolding her brother all the time, and Daddy was even worse when he was home. Now Josh had to go to a dumb school where a dumb teacher was yelling at him, too.

"I don't like that dumb school," she said petulantly.

3

"I don't want you to go!"

"I don't want to go either, but Mom and Dad make me."

"Then Mom and Dad are dumb!"

"No they're not, Ani. If they don't make me go, they get in trouble. It's the law."

"Then the law is dumb!" Anica was starting to cry. Joshua abandoned his ice cream and walked around the table to comfort his sister. He put his arms around her and hugged her tightly. Anica buried her face in his chest and they held each other until her tears were gone.

"You go to kindergarten next year," Joshua told her. "Then we can go together."

"I want to punch your dumb teacher in her dumb face!"

"I get a different teacher next year. Maybe it will be better."

"I still think that school is dumb."

Agnes Miller listened to her children from the next room. She peeked in when she heard Anica crying, and there was Joshua, already holding her close. It was always so touching, seeing the two of them like this.

The first time Joshua saw his sister, he was a little over two years old. Agnes's mother and her sister Alice brought him to the hospital where Agnes was recovering from her C section and Anica lay in an incubator.

Joshua was overjoyed to be with his mother, but he really wanted her to come home. She reassured him that she just needed to stay for a couple of days, and then she would be home, but he would have to help her get better. That reassured him, but when he saw his preemie sister, lying in an incubator, he cried.

"Is Ani going to die?" he asked his aunt, who was a nurse at the hospital.

Alice smiled. "No, Honey, she just needs to grow a little more before she can come home. She'll be just fine, you'll see!"

The nurses would not let Joshua touch her, but he stood by her incubator, studying her tiny face and talking to her. He did not want to leave the neonatal unit when they told him he had to go, and he threw a terrible fit. He wanted to see her every day. Alice would take him to the neonatal unit – if he promised to behave – while his father visited with his mother.

Alice had a little pull with the nurses in the neonatal unit. She took Joshua into the washroom with her and washed his hands extra clean, up to the elbows. She gave him a face mask and made sure he knew how to use it. Then, for a few moments, Joshua was allowed to touch Anica's hand. Her fingers grasped his, and she did not let go. Neither of them would recall this moment, but a tear fell from Alice's eye. She had no children of her own, and it was not likely she ever would. This memory of her nephew and niece would stay with her until her dying day.

When Anica was finally able to come home, Joshua spent every minute he could with her, just sitting on the floor next to her crib. He insisted on being in the same room with her when he took his naps, and it upset him that his parents would not let him share a bedroom with her. He did not understand that babies woke at all hours of the night.

When Anica started to talk, her first word was "Joss." When she could walk, she followed him everywhere, and it delighted Joshua whenever he could do something to make her laugh. When she cried, he would stop at nothing to make her feel better, just as he did now over their melting ice cream.

Agnes wanted to cry herself. John had called and said he was working late and he wouldn't be home for dinner. That meant he wouldn't be home in time to say goodnight to his children, either, just like last night and the night before.

Josh and Ani hadn't even seen their father since Sunday, the one day John never worked, and they didn't see much of him then. He stayed at church to teach a Bible study class while she and the children went to her mother's. When they got home, John sat in the living room with the Sunday paper. He did not even look up when they came in.

Joshua had given up on his father a long time ago, but Anica stood by the side of his chair, her beautiful brown eyes pleading to be noticed. John wordlessly took out the funny papers and gave them to her, then went back to his reading. Anica took them to share with Joshua, but the disappointment in her face broke Agnes's heart.

Anica started to smile again as she and her brother spread out the comics and read them together, lying side by side on their tummies.

At least they have each other, Agnes thought, even though it was already evident that their lives were taking different paths. Anica's future looked brighter every day. Joshua had been struggling in school since the day he started kindergarten. How could two children who were so close be so different? How could two children who were so different be so close? The bond between them was the only thing that gave Joshua any respite from his struggles, and the only thing that eased the heartbreak of Anica's relationship with her father.

Agnes's thoughts turned to the day, just over a year before, that they were first separated, the day when their lives diverged.

Anica

"Joss, don't go!" Anica held her brother tightly in her arms at the entrance to Lincolncrest Elementary School. Joshua held her in his own, doing his best to comfort her, although in truth he would rather just get back in Mom's car and go home with her. She was inconsolable, crying hysterically. Agnes knelt beside them, holding them both.

"Ani, sweetie, it's just for a little while. Josh will come out of those doors in the afternoon, and I'll take you both to Baskin Robbins."

"Why does Joss have to go to kiddygarden anyway?"

"Well, sweetie, it's like I told you. Josh is five years old now. When children are five, they go to kindergarten. Everybody does. It's when we start getting our education. You'll go too when you're five."

Anica's crying diminished a little. "Does that mean I can go to kiddygarden with Joss?"

"Well, no, sweetie, when you go to kindergarten, Josh will be in the second grade. But he'll still be here in this school with you. You can go to school together and walk home together, too." Agnes could tell that her daughter had comprehended little of that. A bell rang. The children queued outside the building began to file in.

8

"Ani, dear, Josh has to go inside now." Anica did not let go of her brother. The queue outside the school systematically shrank. Regretting it even as she said it, Agnes snapped, "Ani! Let your brother go!" Agnes rarely had to raise her voice with her daughter, and never had she done so in circumstances like this. She realized that she could no longer shelter her from all of life's harsh realities, but even so, the memory of her tiny, fragile, and beautiful face, seen through the polycarbonate of her incubator, presented itself. It was all she could do hold herself together.

Anica was visibly wounded, but being the good child that she always was, she let go of Joshua, and with a final, sorrowful look, he turned to line up with the other members of his kindergarten class. Anica watched tearfully as the doors of Lincolncrest Elementary School swallowed him.

Agnes gathered Anica into her arms, picking her up and holding her tightly as she wept. When her sobs subsided, she took her home and tried to engage her in something fun, but she pouted and insisted that she could not have any fun without her brother. Not knowing what else to do, she switched on the TV and changed the channels until she found Spongebob Squarepants. She sat on the sofa watching with her daughter until it was time for her nap. By then, Anica's head was already in her lap and her eyes were droopy. She allowed her to fall asleep like that and sat

9

with her until she woke up.

Anica's mood brightened after her nap, and she played games with her mother until it was time for lunch. Agnes made tomato soup and grilled cheese sandwiches, Anica's favorite – Joshua's too – and set the table for herself and her daughter.

"Why isn't Joss here?" Anica demanded.

"He eats lunch at school with the other children, sweetie."

Anica began to cry again and pushed her plate away. Agnes tried to console her, but she was having none of it. She hadn't had a tantrum since she was barely out of diapers, but she was having one now. Agnes knelt beside her chair until her daughter's fit subsided. She mopped up Anica's face with Kleenex and put their food in the microwave. They ate lunch together, and returned to playing until it was time to pick up Joshua at school.

Anica waited with her mother outside the doors of Lincolncrest Elementary School, watching furtively for her brother. When he emerged, she ran to him. When he saw her, he ran to her and they nearly knocked one another down when they met. The other children regarded them with puzzled smiles. Other parents looked on, clearly moved by the joy unfolding in front of them.

Hand in hand, Josh and Ani ran toward their mother. They happily climbed into the back seat of her

10

Toyota, and once they were snugged into their booster seats, they departed for Baskin Robbins.

Joshua said nothing about his day, and Anica did not ask. They sat close together in the booth across from their mother, Anica with her chocolate sundae and Joshua with his root beer float. The slurping noises Joshua made with his straw were making Anica laugh, and they both seemed happy.

All was well until the next morning when it was time to drop Joshua off at school again. The heart-wrenching scene from the previous day played itself out almost as dramatically. Agnes did not have to snap at Anica quite so harshly, but she still did not want to let her brother go.

Agnes caught a break on the way back from school. A family had recently moved into the house two doors down the street from the Miller home, and they had a little girl named Jessica who was Anica's age. The two girls took an instant liking to one another, and today, Jessica and her mother were gardening in the front yard when they got home. Anica's mood brightened immediately when she spotted her new friend. When Agnes parked the car, she and Anica walked over to say hello.

The two little girls started playing together as soon as they caught sight of each other. Jessica had a little playhouse set up on the front stoop of the house, and there, they happily engaged in make-believe. It was a relief for Agnes to see her daughter so happy after the struggles of the last two mornings.

Ellen Liang took a break from her gardening to bring out some lawn chairs from the garage. Agnes agreed to keep an eye on the children while Ellen went inside to make some tea.

The Liang family were first generation Chinese Americans who had moved to Glen Park for a job opportunity. They had another daughter, Joanna, who was one year older than Jessica. She came outside with Ellen and an older woman when Ellen returned with the tea.

"Agnes, this is my mother, Su Ling. She's visiting from California to help us get settled in."

Ellen spoke in Mandarin to her mother, who smiled at Agnes in return.

"I am happy to meet you, Su Ling," Agnes said graciously. The three women sipped their tea and talked, with Ellen translating for her mother.

What a lovely family, Agnes thought. She wished her own mother could come to help out, but she had suffered a stroke not long after Joshua was born and could not get around well by herself. Agnes's sister Alice lived with her to do the housekeeping and shopping, and to provide companionship.

Alice helped Agnes out when she could, but it was less than what she needed. Agnes's other sister Adele was battling cancer and could not provide much help, either. Her older brother Aaron lived in Houston. Her younger brother Alan had lost a leg in Afghanistan and had enrolled at Texas A&M after he left Walter Reed. He married a girl he met there, and they had a daughter, Julianne, who was the same age as Anica.

If anything, Agnes wished she could spend more time helping her mother and her siblings rather than the other way around. At least there was enough money.

"Mom has to go back to Los Angeles in a few days," Ellen told Agnes. "She's been a godsend, with all the unpacking and settling we've had to do. The girls start preschool tomorrow, thank God."

Preschool. Agnes had not enrolled Joshua when he was three because he stubbornly refused to leave his infant sister. But now that he was in kindergarten, Agnes thought it would be a good idea for Anica – especially if she could go with friends. She and the two Liang girls were having a lot of fun, and it was obviously distracting her from her attachment to her brother.

"Where are you sending them?" Agnes inquired. "Do you think they still have openings?"

"Morningstar Academy over on Sullivan Street. They have a Montessori preschool there. They're a little expensive, but all of their staff are college educated and very nice. I could take you and Ani over there today if you'd like to check it out. My girls can't

13

wait to start."

"Ellen, that would be lovely of you! Thank you so much."

Expensive. Agnes fortunately didn't have to worry about that. John was tight with money, but her mother was not, and she was always eager to help out with the children any way that she could.

Ellen had a big Hyundai minivan that they all piled into, Agnes, Ellen, Su Ling, Anica, Jessica, and Joanna. The school was only a few blocks from home, which Agnes thought was perfect. When they arrived, Anica's eyes grew wide at the sight of all the things they had to do there.

Ellen took Agnes and Su Ling into the office. A woman named Janice greeted them and said cheerful hellos to the three little girls, who she told were welcome to go in and play with the other children. The main room was a happy riot. There were toys of every description everywhere, and many more in bins on the shelves lining the walls. Anica and her two new friends ran in to play.

"Mrs. Miller, you're very lucky. We didn't have any openings here at Morningstar, but one of our families is relocating to the north suburbs, and a slot opened up just this morning. Now, I'm not trying to pressure you, but I would recommend enrolling your daughter now. The opening won't last long."

Agnes looked into the big room. Anica had already

found something and someone to play with and she was very happy. She did not hesitate to enroll her on the spot.

The morning that followed her first day at preschool, Anica just gave her brother a big hug when Agnes dropped him off. Ellen let her ride with her two daughters to the preschool, and Agnes picked all of them up in return. Anica was still overjoyed when they went to pick up Joshua, but she hadn't complained even once.

Preschool was only a few hours a day, but it gave Agnes a great deal of relief from her day-to-day problems. She had tea occasionally with Ellen, but most days, she just indulged in the guilty pleasures of taking baths or watching Oprah without interruptions. She adored her children, but she got too little time for herself.

Anica was excited and intrigued by her new environment. She had never been together with so many other children before. It was a little scary at first, so she stayed close to Jessica and Joanna, but before long, she made many more friends there. The girls liked her immediately. The boys – they were bashful around her, but one of the teachers there told her it was just the way boys are. She omitted the part about it being how they are around pretty girls.

Morningstar was more than a preschool, it was an alternative school for gifted and talented children. The older kids were in another building, but she got to see and mingle with them when they played outside. One day, she saw a girl around six years old doing cartwheels on the grass. Anica watched her intently, and decided to try it for herself. She was clumsy at first, but it did not take her long to catch on. Sandy, a young woman who had been a gymnast as a girl, started giving her assists, and soon, Anica was doing them as well as the older girls there.

Sandy demonstrated some simple exercises for her, including a backbend and a headstand. She offered to teach them to Anica, and she eagerly assented. It did not take her long to master them. Anica was extremely bright, inquisitive, and energetic. She got a lot of notice from the staff and children alike.

Autumn brought cooler weather, and the children spent more time playing indoors. Anica was especially interested in one of the toys in the big room, a brightly painted toy piano, one with two full octaves of white and black keys. It was a bit battered, and a boy named James was always playing with it, slapping the keys and making awful, cacophonous sounds. Anica stood by patiently, hoping he would give it up and play with something else, but he grew possessive of it when she was near. A teacher noticed, and politely asked him to let Anica play with it, but he became indignant. Anica wanted no part of this, so she found Jessica and started playing with her.

Some time later, Anica was surprised when the boy, of his own volition, came over to her with the piano and presented it to her. She looked at him with her big, brown eyes, smiled at him and told him, "Thank you, James." The boy became bashful and ran away, but not before returning a red-faced smile of his own.

Anica sat cross-legged with the little piano in front of her. She methodically pressed each of the twenty-four keys in order, starting with the white keys and moving on to the black ones. Those were in a pattern of twos and threes, and Anica saw that keys that were alike in the pattern played the same notes. Using the black keys as a guide, she found that the white keys did the same. This was a toy for making music! She liked music.

Remembering the ABC song, she started experimenting with the keys until she found the ones she needed to play it. She got good at it very quickly, then she tried playing it with both hands, an octave apart. That was a little harder. She decided she should do it with one hand at a time before trying them together, and that worked. She moved on to "Wheels On The Bus," and before long, she had that down pat, too.

A few of the other children came to listen to her play. One of them was James. Anica smiled at him and offered him the piano, but he shook his head and told her "you play." Anica had found her first fan.

At the end of Anica's third month at Morningstar, the director stepped out to talk to Agnes when she came to pick up the girls. "Mrs. Miller, I just wanted to tell you what a joy it is to have Ani here. She's so well-behaved, and we all love her. She's made herself quite popular here. She's quite the little tumbler! One of our supervisors took gymnastics when she was a girl, and she says Ani is a natural. When she turns five, you should enroll her at Glen Park Gymnastics."

Agnes smiled. "She's been doing lots of somersaults and things around the house. She can even do a headstand. Did she learn that here?"

"Yes, Sandy showed her how to do it, and she caught on so quickly! I also have to say it's unusual for us to see a child who has started music lessons at her age. So talented! Are you a musical family?"

"My mother played the piano before her stroke. But we don't have Ani in music lessons. We don't even have a piano. Why did you think so?"

The director took out her phone and showed Agnes some footage of Anica with the toy piano, surrounded by a group of other children. They were singing along with the songs they knew and just listening to the ones they didn't. Anica was playing nursery songs. She was also playing songs she had heard on the radio station Agnes listened to in the car. Agnes was astonished.

That Sunday after church, Agnes asked her mother if Anica could play with the spinet piano she still kept in her living room. It was covered with a lace doily and served as a place to put family photos.

"But of course, dear!" her mother responded. "Heaven knows, I don't play it any more. I'll get it moved to your house for her! Alice, can you open the piano for Ani?"

Anica surveyed her grandmother's piano. So many keys! And the keys were too big! Still, she was drawn to it, and she awkwardly seated herself on the bench. She saw that the black keys repeated the same two-three pattern as her little piano at preschool, and she tested them to see if they made the same notes. She couldn't reach all of them from where she was sitting, but she tested the ones she could reach, and as she expected, they made the same sounds. Most of them were lower in pitch, and some were higher, than the toy piano at Morningstar.

It was hard for her to adjust to the spacing of the keys at first, but she took it slowly. Soon, she was performing "Wheels On The Bus" for her grandmother and her aunt. Joshua looked on, intensely interested. When she was finished with the song, everyone clapped enthusiastically, especially her brother. Then she played the melody of a Taylor Swift song that had been on the radio a lot. Grandma and Alice were incredulous, while Joshua swayed to the music.

The following Monday, when Agnes came to pick up Anica and the Liang girls, the director met her, accompanied by two other women Agnes had not met before.

"Mrs. Miller, I'd like you to meet Nicole Warmowski, our music teacher. And this is Tatyana Ilyanovich. Mrs. Ilyanovich is also a music teacher." The women smiled and greeted Agnes. "Nicky, can you tell Mrs. Miller what Ani has been doing for us?"

"It's nice to meet you, Mrs. Miller. As you know, we here at Morningstar work with a lot of special children, and little Ani is certainly special. Janice showed me the videos she made of Ani playing our little toy piano, and I asked her if I could send them to Tatyana. I hope you don't mind. Tatyana is a concert pianist and a graduate of the Moscow Conservatory in Russia. She teaches special children like your daughter."

Tatyana was an attractive woman in her late forties. She spoke, smiling warmly. "Mrs. Miller, I invite you and Ani come to my house. It not far from here. I have nice Steinway piano I think Ani will like."

Agnes did not know what to make of this. Still – she seemed nice enough, even if she was a little hard to understand, and she trusted the judgment of the staff at Morningstar. She told Tatyana she had to take the Liang girls home, but she could come afterwards.

The Ilyanovich home was lovely. It was not a big house, and it might have looked cluttered were everything not meticulously in its place. There was a wall full of diplomas, some in Russian, some in French, some in English. The living room's most prominent features were three pianos – two impressive studio grands and an electronic instrument connected to a computer. One corner held a glass-doored cabinet stacked with recording equipment.

Anica looked around with a sense of wonder. She had never seen such a place. Everything was so interesting! She began to wander the room to explore, examining everything, and touching many things. Agnes admonished her daughter to be careful.

"Is okay, Mrs. Miller. Is place for children." Tatyana laughed a little. "You like tea? I make some. I have cookies and milk for Ani if okay."

Agnes told her that would be lovely. "Tatyana – may I call you Tatyana? – why the interest in Ani? I know she's very bright, but she's just a little girl, hardly more than a baby."

"I show you." Tatyana said, smiling. She touched Anica gently and invited her to sit down at one of the two grand pianos. Tatyana sat at the other one. "Ani, *solnyshka*, we play game! Listen what I play, then you play, okay?" Tatyana played a few bars of a simple melody on her piano. Anica repeated it perfectly on hers. She played the same melody again, this time all the way through. Once again, Anica repeated it perfectly.

"Very good, Ani! Go back with mother now.

Maybe we play again soon, okay?" Anica beamed at her as she returned to the sofa to join her mother. Tatyana rose from her piano and took a small chocolate, ornately wrapped in foil with Cyrillic letters on it, from a dish on a bookcase nearby.

"Okay for daughter to have candy?" she asked Agnes. Agnes nodded, and Anica delightedly unwrapped the delicacy Tatyana gave her. Tatyana sat down on the sofa with Agnes. She still smiled, but she had a serious look in her eyes.

"Anica is prodigy," she told her. "Song I play, children sing in Vologda, where I from. No one knows here. She listen one time, play perfectly." Tatyana gestured to the piano where her daughter had sat. "She must learn this. Start now. I teach her."

"I don't know, Tatyana. I'll have to talk to my husband. He worries about money." This was true. John had been unhappy about his mother-in-law paying for Anica's preschool, but he would never have agreed to pay Morningstar's tuition, and it was obviously a good experience for her daughter.

Tatyana smiled. "Anica must know this. You see, she already love it. I will teach her. Pay what you can pay, money not important. Child important. Very important."

Agnes told Tatyana she would need a few days to think about it. She collected her daughter and drove directly to Lincolncrest Elementary, as it was nearly time to pick up Joshua.

As always, Anica and her brother ran to each other and joyfully embraced. Anica reached into the pocket of her jumper and gave Joshua another of the Russian chocolates Tatyana had given her. It had gotten slightly smashed on the way there, but Joshua was delighted anyway. "Nice lady gave me this for you," she told him.

With her children playing happily in the family room, Agnes looked up "Tatyana Ilyanovich" on the computer. What she found astonished her. There were scores of pictures of her. In one of them, she posed next to Daniel Barenboim, principal conductor of the Chicago Symphony. In others, she sat at large pianos in concert venues around the world. In others, she posed with children of all ages, who were often dressed formally, seated at other large pianos in other concert venues. She had music on iTunes and Amazon, and quite a few videos on YouTube. Although Agnes knew little about classical music, she watched some of them and was extremely impressed.

There was a Wikipedia page with an extensive biography of her. She had been an up-and-coming concert pianist before she emigrated to the U.S., but she wanted to marry and have children. Touring became too stressful for her, so she now devoted her time to teaching exceptionally talented children. Agnes was humbled.

The next day, she talked to her daughter. "Ani, did you like Mrs. Ilyanovich? The woman with the pianos? Do you think you want to go there again?" Anica's eyes lit up.

"Can we go there today, Mommy?"

Joshua

The sounds of his sister's sobs stayed in his ears as Joshua's class filed into the building. This was a scary place, and he didn't know any of the other children. He felt lost, being separated from her.

A plump woman in her middle thirties had stood at the head of the queue he joined outside of the school, and she now greeted each child at the door of a brightly lit classroom. She asked him his name. Joshua was too overwhelmed by all of the new things that presented themselves to his sight to be aware of her at first. She touched his shoulder, startling him, and asked him again.

"J-Joshua. Joshua Miller."

The woman smiled. "Hello, Joshua, I'm Mrs. Kerrigan and I'll be your teacher this year. Welcome to kindergarten. Let's see … ah, your seat is right over there." She pointed to an empty chair at a table where there were two girls and a scruffy-looking boy. Joshua ambled over and sat down. His surroundings grew more frightening each time he looked around the room. Panic rose in him and he left his seat, running tearfully towards the door. Mrs. Kerrigan stopped him.

"Joshua? What's wrong, sweetie?

"Ani," Joshua sobbed. "I need to see Ani!"

"You'll have to wait until after school, dear. This is school. This is where you're supposed to be right now."

"Please let me see my sister! Please!" Joshua's pleas grew more strident, prompting Mrs. Kerrigan to take him into the hall.

"Joshua!" Mrs. Kerrigan said sternly, "You're almost six years old! You have to go to school now. You go to school with children your own age. Do you understand?"

"Why can't Ani come with me?"

Mrs. Kerrigan's tone softened. "Joshua, honey, your sister is too young for kindergarten. She can't come here until she's your age. Now listen, there are lots of children inside who want to be your friends. Why don't you go inside and join them."

"Okay," Joshua said meekly. She escorted him back into the classroom and he took his seat. All of the other children were looking at him. He was growing fearful again when the scruffy boy next to him spoke up.

"Kinda sucks, huh?" he said. Joshua studied him. His dark hair was long, but not as long as most of the girls', and it looked like it had been cut with hedge trimmers. His jeans had holes in the knees and his dirty sneakers had a hole in one toe. He wore a ragged T-shirt that was too big on him. In its center was a faded picture of a human skull wearing a garland of roses. It was more funny than scary, and there was something about this boy that made him feel more at

26

ease.

"Hi," he said. "I'm Kevin. Kevin Maas."

Joshua managed a smile. "Joshua Miller. You can call me Josh."

"Hey, Josh." Kevin offered his hand and Joshua took it. "You know something?" Kevin said in a low voice. "I got a sister, too, but she's a lot older than me and I'm glad she's not here!"

"Kevin? Joshua? Class is about to begin, be quiet, please!" Mrs. Kerrigan scolded.

The two boys grinned at each other. Joshua stammered and stumbled through his first day of school, but having Kevin there made it easier. Nevertheless, he was overjoyed when school was finally over and he saw Anica running up the walk to greet him. Everything was all right now. Joshua did not stop to ponder that every day for the next thirteen years might be like this one.

The next day at kindergarten was better, because he now knew where he was supposed to be, and Kevin was there next to him, as friendly and easygoing as he was the day before. Joshua liked the T-shirt he wore better than the first one he'd seen. There was a triangle in the middle and something like a rainbow coming out of one side. It was pretty. Joshua asked about it.

"Pink Floyd," Kevin told him. "My dad listens to them all the time." Joshua couldn't understand. There was no pink on the shirt and the name Floyd wasn't plural. No matter, he liked the shirt and he liked Kevin more with each passing day. The other children in the room were not so friendly to either of them, so it was good that they had found each other. Joshua had never had a friend before, but he was so close to Anica he didn't know he needed one.

Here in this overwhelming place, he definitely needed one. Mrs. Kerrigan was constantly shushing them when they were supposed to be doing something else. They would both chuckle it off, but it was a lot easier for Kevin to understand what they were supposed to be doing after they had been shushed. When Joshua felt lost, which was all of the time, he'd ask Kevin for help, but Mrs. Kerrigan would shush them again and would come over to get Joshua on track. Except for Kevin, the other children found this amusing.

After a few days, saying goodbye to his sister in the morning got much easier. Their reunions in the afternoon were just as happy, but Anica was full of talk about Miss Janice and Miss Sandy and all of the neat stuff they had at Morningstar Academy. Joshua was a bit jealous, not of his beloved sister, but of how nice she made it sound compared to what he was going through in kindergarten. He longed to join her.

A couple of months passed. The weather turned colder and nastier. One day, Anica started to tell him about a nice lady with a name he could not pronounce

– but he soon learned to like the little chocolates his sister brought with her when she'd visited her.

Around the same time, a couple of big men in gray overalls came through the door carrying Grandma's piano, and then a guy with a lot of strange tools took it apart, fixed a bunch of stuff, and spent a couple of hours tuning it.

Joshua found it both puzzling and fascinating, but he loved it when Anica would climb up onto the bench and start making music with it. Joshua wanted to join in, but his mother told him it was something Anica had to do by herself, so he contented himself with listening. Before long, a lot of the stuff she played was boring, just notes going up and down and some stuff that was simpler than what she already knew how to play. He soon learned to find something else to do when she practiced. It was never for very long, and she always came to find him when it was over.

Kindergarten grew more challenging. Even when Joshua understood the stuff he was supposed to be doing, a lot of it seemed pointless to him. He thought it was neat the first time he learned how to use Elmer's Glue, but the repetition soon became tedious.

There was little more he could do with crayons, either. They made lots of different colors, and he could put together things he kind of liked, but sitting next to Kevin – the things he was producing were really interesting. Sometimes they were pretty, sometimes they were funny, but they were never boring. Mrs. Kerrigan put some of the pretty ones up on the bulletin boards and scolded him for the really funny ones Joshua liked.

One gray Wednesday in late October, Mrs. Kerrigan gave Joshua a piece of paper she instructed him to give to his parents. It was raining and cold when his mother came to pick him up. Joshua held the paper over his head to shelter himself from the rain, then he dutifully handed it to his mother when he got in the car. Weather like this meant hot chocolate at home, and he and his sister chatted happily while they sipped.

It was alarming to both of them when their mother came in, still clutching the paper Mrs. Kerrigan had given Joshua. She tried to smile and pretend nothing was wrong, but both Joshua and Anica knew otherwise.

Neither of them would hear the heated argument that ensued when their father got home because they were both asleep. Joshua never learned what Mrs. Kerrigan had written on that paper, but after that, his mother seemed sadder, if more attentive of him, and his father seemed more distant. Joshua concluded there must be something wrong with him, but at least Anica did not think so. The happy reunions after school continued until Anica turned five and was able to go to kindergarten at Lincolncrest Elementary School. Then they got to walk home together, but only part of the time. She saw her piano teacher twice a week now, and Mom had enrolled her in gymnastics.

By and by, more notes came home from Joshua's teachers, and there was more sadness on his mother's face, more heated arguments between his parents that Joshua sometimes heard now. Anica would fall asleep as soon as her head hit the pillow, but Joshua often lay awake, listening to the muffled sounds of his parents talking about him.

Kindergarten, first grade, second grade – the only constants were the scowls on the faces of his teachers, his parents' arguments, and his sister's unquestioning love. After kindergarten, someone at the school had decided it would be better if he and Kevin were not in class together, but Joshua still laughed at the drawings he made when they sat down together for lunch. When third grade came along, things really started to change, and not for the better.

Another gray Wednesday. Wednesday was piano, so Joshua had to walk home from school without his sister. Four lonely blocks – no, make that six. He spied Jesse Duncan lurking on the next corner and changed direction to avoid him.

"Hey, Miller! Where's your baby sister today?"

Crap, Joshua thought, *he saw me.* It was bad enough having to sit next to him all day, enduring the endless indignities he inflicted when Mrs. Marcus wasn't looking. There was a history quiz today, something about the Massachusetts Bay Colony. Joshua finished less than half of it before time ran out. Jesse did even less, maybe because he spent more time looking at Joshua's paper than his own.

The only thing Joshua liked about Jesse Duncan was that he was the one kid in class who was stupider than he was. The rest of him – he had a good four inches and twenty-five pounds on Joshua. His older brother was an all-district linebacker at Glen Park Central High, and their six-foot-four-inch father drove them around in a big Ford F-350 pickup truck. All three of them wore their hair in the same bristly crew cut, and they all had the same rotten personality.

"Go away, Jesse," Joshua muttered.

"Who's gonna make me? Your mama? Or maybe your cute little sister will rescue you!"

"Hey, Jesse, leave my sister alone. She's only six years old."

"I'll bet she's a good kisser. Maybe I'll kiss her."

Joshua was mad enough to punch Jesse in the face, but he knew he'd end up with a broken arm if he tried. He walked doggedly on, trying to ignore his taunts and insults. He was relieved when the enormous pickup belonging to Jesse's father pulled alongside them. His father rolled his window down.

"Jess, come on. Let's go watch your brother practice."

"See ya tomorrow, Miller. And bring your baby sister along." As Jesse turned to go, he made vulgar kissing noises with his lips. Jesse got in the truck with his father, who smirked at Joshua as he rolled up his window. The truck rumbled away, leaving Joshua choking on diesel fumes.

Joshua was dejected the rest of the way home. Why couldn't he walk with Ani on Wednesdays? Let's see, Mondays and Wednesdays her piano teacher picked her up. Tuesdays and Thursdays, she hitched a ride with another girl in her gymnastics class. The only day they could walk home together was Friday, and Anica had told him her coach wanted her to start coming to practice on Fridays, too.

They didn't even walk to school together any more. Anica's friend Jessica lived two doors down from them, and she walked with her and her sister now. Joshua would tag along, but he kept a respectable distance because kids like Jesse would come down even harder on him if they saw him walking with a bunch of girls.

In spite of Jesse's bravado, he never bothered Joshua when he was with Anica. Anica wasn't a loser like him, and bullies like Jesse had some kind of honor code where they would only pick on the losers, Joshua thought glumly.

At least he had Kevin to talk to at lunch. Like Joshua, Kevin was not very popular, but unlike Joshua, he didn't care. His hair was long, his jeans were frayed, and he wore oversized T-shirts with the names of old rock bands like Black Sabbath on them. His parents were just as eccentric as he was, but Joshua often felt more comfortable at their house than at his own.

It was too bad that he lived in the opposite direction from school, so they couldn't walk together. Kevin had to catch a bus to afterschool care every day anyway because his parents both worked. Kevin's father taught fine arts at a local college, and his mother was a yoga instructor.

Anica loved school and it seemed to him that all she could talk about when they did walk together was how much fun she'd had that day, and how nice her teacher was. To Joshua, school was a prison camp, which left him with little to tell his sister. When she wasn't talking about school, she might tell him about how exciting it was to be a Level Three gymnast after just one year of training. Or how her piano teacher, a lady with a Russian accent and an unpronounceable name, told her she was a prodigy who would be playing Tchaikovsky concertos before she entered high school.

Joshua still adored his sister, but they had so little in common now, and they did so little together. When Anica got home from her activities, she would promptly do her homework. Then she would sit at the piano Grandma had given her, and practice until dinnertime. After dinner there would be more practice, and maybe some flexibility exercises, and then it would be time for bed.

She'd made a lot of friends and was spending time with them, too. On Saturdays, she had more gymnastics, or maybe a recital, and frequent playdates and sleepovers with her friends. His parents sat between them at church – Joshua and his sister both hated church, and being unable to sit together made it worse.

All Joshua could count on was a little time together on Sundays, and walking home together on Fridays. Friday afternoon was still special. Anica told her friends she really liked walking with her brother on Fridays, and it kept them connected even if they didn't have a lot to talk about. If she caved in to her coach and started going to gymnastics on Friday, he would lose even that. He would almost certainly lose that, he thought, because once Anica got to Level Four, she would be invited to join the team. Joshua could never allow himself to come between her and that.

Jesse Duncan infuriated him. Mrs. Marcus knew what a jerk he was, but she let him get away with it most of the time. If anything, she came down harder on Joshua, embarrassing him in front of his classmates. He wasn't aware that his teacher knew he had the aptitude to do much better in school, while

Jesse was just plain dim. The hardest part was the way the other kids treated him. They would sometimes laugh when Mrs. Marcus prodded him about something, and they saw what went on between Jesse and him even when Mrs. Marcus didn't.

Then there was the new girl, Becky. Joshua thought she was the prettiest girl he'd ever seen, maybe the prettiest girl in the world, even. He was ashamed of how stupid and disliked he was. He would never be able to talk to her. He gazed at her longingly, but he would quickly avert his unworthy eyes if he thought she might catch him doing it.

She sat at the table behind him with two other pretty girls and a quiet boy who wore glasses. When homework was handed forward, hers would be on top, and even her handwriting was pretty. She dotted her i's with little circles, and he thought he could smell strawberries on her paper. Her mother was very pretty, too, and she drove Becky to and from school in a flashy Mercedes convertible every day. Not just pretty, but rich, too, he thought bitterly. He would never know her. She probably couldn't even see him, and she never would.

Mom would be home when he got there. When she asked him about his day, he would just say it was "fine" or "good," and he evaded any pressure for details. Mom was all right. She sometimes scolded him about his room or his chores, but she was never really mad at him. Sometimes he wished he could tell her about how things really were for him at school, but that meant she would tell his father, and his father never had anything good to say to him.

Dad would just tell him his teacher would let up on him if he'd just do his work instead of daydreaming all the time. If his teacher let up on him, then the other kids would, too. If he told him what a jerk Jesse was, he'd tell him to punch him in the nose. That was when his father was in a good mood. When he wasn't, he'd start ranting about how he was a lazy bum who would never amount to anything.

Summers were better. There was no homework, no teachers to scold him. He still got to spend very little time with his sister. When Anica started school, their mother went back to work part time at the construction company where she had worked before he was born. Joshua went to day camps all summer long. Anica went to gymnastics camp, day after day, and she kept getting better and better. She still had her piano lessons twice a week, and she still practiced every day. She kept getting better and better at that, too, which meant more and more practice.

When fourth grade came for Joshua, surely enough, Anica had been promoted to Level Four and she was invited to join the team. Nine hours of practice during the week, and four hours on Saturdays. There was still Sunday at Grandma's, but a lot of the time Grandma and Aunt Alice would talk her ear off about how proud of her they were, or about how pretty she looked, while Joshua might as well have been a ghost. Joshua was proud of his sister, but he envied the attention she was getting. Ani was so successful, so happy, while his life was just getting worse.

Neither Jesse nor Becky were in class with him this year. He would still gaze at Becky during recess and lunch. Jesse would still ambush him on his way home from school, but he'd gone out for sports this year and practice kept him out of Joshua's hair a lot of the time.

It wasn't of much comfort. The work at school just kept getting harder and harder, and he was getting more homework. He tried to do the work, but he couldn't concentrate. His attention in class would wander. Sometimes he would study the maps on the wall, or look out of the windows when he was supposed to be taking a quiz or reading something. He would start on his homework, but he quickly grew frustrated and gave up. Asking mom for help would mean even more lectures from his father. Why couldn't she just keep mum about it?

His favorite diversion was mechanical things. He enjoyed taking apart broken appliances and putting them back together to see how they worked. Once, he actually got one of his mother's cast-off hair dryers to work after he found a loose connection in the wiring. His mother was pleased when he presented it to her, but she followed it up by asking if all his homework was done. It was not, so he unhappily slinked off to his room to take another crack at his math worksheet. He just started writing down gibberish for the ones he could not even start on. It would be enough to fool his mother, but he could hardly hand it in that way. He'd tell the teacher he lost it or forgot it, but he knew she didn't believe him.

As life got harder for him, he withdrew, saying less and less and spending most of his time in his room. He resigned himself to the derision he would get from his father and his teachers. The laughing and taunting he got from the other kids turned into a monotonous din that wasn't too hard to push out of his head.

Anica just continued to rack up awards and accolades, excelling in school, winning medals and trophies, and bowing to the enthusiastic applause she received at her recitals. Why had they turned out to be so different? Why couldn't she just give some of it up so he would have someone to love him again, someone who would not judge him?

Today was yet another gray Wednesday. Another piano day. Anica got home earlier on piano days, but it made little difference in the time she had for him. Joshua still waited for her to come in and hug him before she got busy with practice. Just a moment of closeness, of sweetness, then she would sit down with her music and begin her warmups. Why did she have to warm up when she'd just come home from her lesson, he wondered. Anica told him it was because that was what she was supposed to do before every practice.

It seemed to him that Anica's life was like that now. Always doing what she was supposed to do. And all of it meant she was supposed to spend more time away from her brother. What was he supposed to do? There was no end to the nagging, scolding, and lecturing he got, but none of it instilled in him a sense of purpose. Was that to be the purpose of his life, to acquiesce, just to be nagged, scolded, and lectured about something else? It made him want to retreat to his room, to his tinkering, to his daydreaming, while people with purpose in their lives went on, leaving him behind.

Sometimes he thought he should run away. He gave no thought to what a kid like him could do without any money, without anywhere to go. He only wanted to stop the pain, but how could he leave Ani?

The third week of October, midterm report cards were issued. Through the third grade, Joshua had managed to stay in the "improvement needed" category in most of his subjects. This term, he was marked as "intervention needed" in math and language arts. This was elementary school jargon for "failing."

Joshua numbly gave the envelope to his mother. She never went too hard on him; she just told him that he could do better. When she saw his marks this time, she buried her face in her hands and started to cry.

"I'm sorry, Mom," Joshua said meekly. He was surprised at her response. She embraced him tightly, then went back to her sobbing. Not knowing what more he could say to her, he went to his room, where he would lie on his bed until his father came home. He dreaded that moment, and when it came, his dread was justified.

"Intervention needed?" The anger in his father's voice was palpable. "What does this mean, Joshua? What? Have you paid attention at all this year, or did they put you so close to the window you've taken up bird watching? What is wrong with you? What? When I was your age, my father worked me past sundown after I got home from school, but I still managed to get my lessons done. What do you even do when you get home from school? Your room is a pigsty. The wastebasket under the sink is still full. You know that's your job!"

Joshua wished he could be anywhere but here. He didn't think he could be torn down any farther, but his father was relentless.

"Listen, boy, the law says I have to take care of you until you're eighteen, then you're out of here, do you understand? And I want you to change your name. You're no Miller! A Miller knows the value of a day's work. You don't even know what work is. You know

41

what, you're going to end up washing cars or busing tables for a living! Or you're going to end up like one of those panhandling bums downtown, sleeping in the alley in a cardboard box. Now get to your room. I don't want to see you the rest of the night!"

Joshua had been banished. Cast out of his own family. His father's words had cut so deep, he could no no longer feel a connection to his mother. He could no longer feel a connection even to Anica. Some part of him knew he didn't deserve this. Why did everyone else get to carry on with their lives, when he had been told his was worthless? His despair was matched only by his anger.

When bedtime arrived, his mother came up to let him out of his room so he could brush his teeth. He passed Anica in the hall. She had overheard their father's tirade, and she tried to embrace him, but he snapped at her.

"So what did you get? 'Greatly exceeds expectations' again? Just like every other time? Aren't you dying to brag about it to Jessica? Did you win another medal this week? Did Mrs. Whatthehellovich give you some more of that fancy Russian candy because you play your piano so pretty? Dad says I never do my homework, but how can I with that godawful noise you make when you practice?"

Anica burst into tears and ran into her room. His mother ran after her. Joshua ran his brush over his teeth a few times, then sullenly padded back to his room. He laid on his bed face down with his head turned away from the door. His mother entered a few minutes later.

"Joshua Miller!" she said harshly. "You get up and apologize to your sister this minute!"

Joshua rose from his bed and left his room to knock on Anica's door. She did not come. When he tried the doorknob, it was locked.

"Ani, I'm sorry," he said through the closed door.

"Just go away, Josh." Joshua could tell from the sound of her voice that she was still crying. He really was sorry for his outburst in the hall, but now he had broken the last good thing he had in his life. No one loved him now, and he didn't think anyone ever would again.

He retreated to his own room, realizing that this was it. He had hit bottom and there was no way up from here. He wondered what it would be like, sleeping behind a dumpster after his father threw him out. He'd turned ten only a week before. It would be eight more years until he turned eighteen. He did not think being a bum could be worse than what he would endure in school and at home with his father, but he did not know if he could live another eight years this way.

He must wall himself off, he thought. If he could build a high enough wall, then perhaps he could

43

endure the time. It would be especially hard to keep Anica out, but it would really be better for her if she could have her wonderful life without a loser like him messing it up for her. There was more than enough for him to be jealous of. He could work with that.

For the most part, he simply withdrew even more. His room became his fortress, where he could close his door, stuff his earbuds into his ears, and shut out the whole world. When he could not avoid Anica altogether, he didn't speak to her. If she spoke to him, he might say, "What's it to you?" Or just, "can't you just leave me alone?"

In time, Anica started to avoid him, too. It just hurt her too much to deal with her brother, the way he'd become. She put more time into her friends and her pursuits. In particular, she spent more time at her piano. Joshua had said it interfered with his homework, but for God's sake, he never did it anyway. It infuriated her that he could blame her for that!

Joshua turned up the volume on his iPad when she practiced, trying to tune her out. She started out with scales and exercises that grated on his nerves. There was always a pause before she started playing any real music.

Once in a while, curiosity got the better of him and he would listen a little. He didn't get it, and he'd return to his game or whatever he was listening to. One day, though, she played something he kind of liked. When she had a new piece to practice, she would play in fits and starts that were almost as annoying as her scales. It was not so with this piece. It was beautiful, haunting. He listened to it all the way through and he hoped she would play it again.

The piece was Beethoven's *Für Elise,* although Joshua had no way of identifying it. When she started again, he quietly crept down the stairs to the landing so he could better hear it, and so he could watch her play.

Her hands floated over the keys in motions as graceful and beautiful as the music itself. He watched and listened until it was over and she began to play another piece he did not like so much, something by J. S. Bach that sounded mechanical to him. He retreated to his room and resumed wasting his time.

When he got home from school the next day, Anica was at gymnastics. He opened her piano and touched some of the keys. He could make sounds, but he could not make music. Anica had left her sheet music on the rack, and Joshua could not understand how she or anyone else could make sense of it. Joshua pressed several of the keys with the palms of his hands, making an awful, dissonant noise that brought his mother in from the kitchen.

"Joshua!" she cried. "Please don't do that to your sister's piano!" Joshua looked into his mother's eyes. Tears were welling in his own.

"Why, Mom? Why is she so smart when I'm so

stupid? I can't do anything!"

Joshua turned and ran up the stairs to his room. His mother followed.

"Joshua, Honey, you're not stupid! You're not! Your sister practices for hours, and she started playing when she was little."

"All I did when I was little was play with her!" Joshua cried bitterly. "I used to think I was at least good at that! I guess I just wasn't good enough for her!"

"Joshua, your sister loves you."

"No she doesn't, Mom! All she loves is her piano and her gymnastics and school and all of her friends!"

Agnes sat on the bed with her son and tried to comfort him, but she didn't know what to say to him. She put her arms around him, but his body remained stiff and tense.

She had to leave because it was time to pick Anica up from gymnastics. She would not know what to say to her, either. Whenever Anica tried to get through to her brother, he pushed her away. After a while, she stopped trying.

Fifth grade played out like a bad sequel to the previous four years, the umptieth iteration of some idiotic slasher flick where everybody knew the killer would return and the victims would stupidly look in the basement.

Joshua was able to scrape by in school only because

of the intervention they said he needed. He was forced to stay after school three days a week while a teacher would go about the room checking his work and that of the other dumb kids. She would stand by his desk, condescendingly walking him through his work, treating him as she might treat a much younger child. It kept his grades marginal, but he didn't feel good about it. It only reinforced his notion of how stupid he was.

When homework hour was over, the streets and sidewalks would be empty of other kids, who were off somewhere not being losers. At least it provided him with a way of avoiding Jesse Duncan. On the days when he was allowed to leave school on time, he left by a different door each day and took a circuitous route to get home. Jesse would still ambush him occasionally, but Joshua learned that if he could just keep his head down for a couple of blocks, Jesse would have his fun and then leave him alone.

He still gazed hopelessly at Becky Lindstrom, who just got prettier every year. The thought that she would never know he was alive no longer depressed him. Seeing her allowed him to feel something that was not black and shapeless like the other things he felt. She was a little ray of sunshine penetrating the canopy of the dark forest he wandered through, trudging towards his eighteenth birthday and life on the streets.

Anica continued to get better at the many things she

did so well. She had lots of friends, and she was
happy. Joshua continued his snipes and insults with
her, and in time, she learned to give as good as she got.
Their mother scolded them both for bickering but she
gave up trying to reconcile the two of them. They
would have to work this out on their own.

In the spring, Joshua and the other fifth graders
were given a tour of Harry S. Truman Junior High
School, where he would go next year. The school was
much bigger than Lincolncrest. The floor plan was
confusing, and there were long, imposing rows of
lockers everywhere. Instead of one teacher, he would
have five, one for each subject. It was scary, Joshua
thought, but he also thought it could not be any worse
than Lincolncrest. He had not learned how to achieve,
but he'd learned how to survive.

Summer arrived. Joshua headed to day camp, while
his sister spent the summer improving and improving
and getting prettier and prettier. They didn't talk
anymore, so she had more time to practice, and he had
more time to spend in his room.

Kevin and his family moved out of the
neighborhood. His new house wasn't too far away, but
he didn't get to see as much of him now. Joshua
missed having him around, but he was so down most
of the time that it didn't seem to make things any
worse.

This summer wasn't the same. Joshua felt strange.

He didn't feel sick or hurt anywhere. He just felt strange, in more ways than one, and these feelings were new to him. They had come on so gradually he didn't think about them, but now he was having them all the time.

His body was changing in ways he didn't understand. He also felt differently when he was around girls. He had always felt a kind of giddy anxiety when he was near the pretty ones. He still felt those things, but there was something else. They ran around in shorts all day at camp, and on pool days, seeing them in their swimsuits drove him crazy. They were undergoing changes, too, but they were easier to understand as he could see them in older girls and women.

He inevitably discovered something that made him feel both very good and very naughty, so naughty that he attempted to stop. He could go no more than a day before he returned to it. It would remain a guilty secret he would have to keep from everyone. Maybe it would go away on its own, or maybe he really was sick with something and he would die.

It did not go away on its own. Joshua did not get sick and he certainly did not die. Even when he began to do it several times a day, he felt no worse. Not long after he discovered this guilty pleasure, he started to grow pubic hair. He was mortified at this development, believing he really was getting sick. But

49

then he remembered that he had seen hair like this before, in the changing room at the pool. Grown men had a lot of it, as well as hair on their chests and elsewhere on their bodies. Joshua was a boy, and boys turned into men. He did not understand exactly how this happened, but he reasoned that his nascent pubic hair was part of the process. Maybe the rest of it was, too.

Maybe Kevin will know, he thought. If Joshua could confide in anyone, it would be him. Joshua asked his mom if she would take him over there on Saturday.

"Yeah, I do it," Kevin told him. "So does everybody else. Even girls do it. Didn't you get that in sex ed?"

"I didn't take sex ed. My father wouldn't let me."

"Didn't he talk to you about it himself? My dad did. He's totally cool with it as long as I keep my door closed."

"My dad would say it's a sin. He thinks everything is a sin.

Kevin chuckled. "That's why we don't go to church. Dad says they're only out for money, anyway."

"I wish I had your mom and dad. Well, maybe just your dad, my mom's all right."

"I wish I had your sister," Kevin lamented. "I want to marry her when I grow up."

"Ani? All she does is play her stupid piano and go

to her stupid gymnastics. She does all of her homework and cleans up her room. Little miss perfect, makes me look like more of a loser than I already am."

"But she's so freakin' beautiful! Doesn't that drive you crazy?"

"Yeah, it drives me crazy. Everybody is always looking at her. Nobody even sees me unless I'm doing something wrong."

"Hey, next Saturday, can I come to your house? I want to see Ani."

"Not funny, Kevin."

Anica

Anica wiped the mist from the bathroom mirror with her towel. She regarded her reflection this way and that. She was slender, lean, and very fair. Her long brown hair hung straight and wet. Her big, brown eyes were wide set and crystal clear.

Am I pretty? she wondered. Everyone told her she was. A lot of the boys at school would act kind of funny around her. Jessica told her boys act like that when they're around girls that they like. Anica thought Jessica was pretty, but Jessica was several months older than she, and she already had a chest.

Her own chest was still flat, which brought her some dismay. Jessica and some of the other girls in her fourth grade class had already started to pop, and she was envious. She was almost ten – she should have started to grow something by now, she thought. Otherwise, she was happy with the way she looked. Gymnastics gave definition to her body and grace to her movements. *How many of those not-so-flat girls can do a double back walkover on a balance beam,* she thought wryly.

She'd won that event at the regionals on Saturday. She got third place on her floor exercise and came in third overall. She was proud of herself, but once again, only her mother and her teammates were there to watch. Joshua had not seen her perform since she was six. Her father had never seen her perform at all. Grandma and Aunt Alice would tell her they were proud of her, but they never got to see her except on video her mother took with her phone. Anica was content doing this mainly for herself, but it would be nice if it wasn't always just Mom in the stands.

When Mom brought her home on Saturday, there was no one there to see the three shiny medals she'd been awarded. Dad was working and Joshua was over at Kevin's house. She went to her room and hung them on a peg underneath her trophy shelf, adding to the dozens of others she kept there. Mom had taken a picture of her wearing them after the meet and sent it to Dad and Aunt Alice. She would hear about it at Grandma's tomorrow, but her father would not mention it.

Anica was a good, regionally competitive gymnast, but she had no illusions about going much farther than that. She loved it, but she was not willing to make the sacrifices necessary to compete at the national level. It would mean giving up music, and she could not do that.

She was very good at playing the piano, so much so that she had placed highly enough to compete at the state level. She had already drawn the attention of some of the better music schools, even Julliard in New York. She had been invited to go to a special school for kids with talent in the performing arts, but she did not want to leave her friends – and her brother, even though they weren't getting along. Besides, she already took lessons from Tatyana Ilyanovich, one of the best music teachers in the country.

Yet it was still just her mother in the audience whenever she played in public. It would mean more to her if her father or her brother came to her recitals. She put emotion into her gymnastics, but it was through her music that she could truly express herself.

She got more notice at school. She was an excellent student, and all of her teachers loved her. She had many friends, and she enjoyed a vibrant social life. She felt a little guilty about that. Her brother was a misfit and an outcast. He'd gone on to middle school this year, which made it a little easier for her. When they had been at Lincolncrest together, she sometimes had to defend Joshua from the derision of some of her friends – even after the falling-out they'd had when she had just started the second grade. She bickered with Joshua at home, but she never thought he was treated fairly at school or even in her own family.

When Joshua's frustration boiled over, he would decry how stupid he thought he was. Anica knew differently. He was the only one in the family who could operate the remotes for the TV and the cable box. He amazed her with his skill at the computer her parents set up for them in the family room. Anica could do little more with it than the things she was taught in school. No one praised him for the things he could do well, but there was no end to the criticism he received for the things he couldn't.

Anica never went there with him. When he insulted her, she snapped at him about his behavior towards her, in the moment. She might say, "that was mean, and you know it!" She might say, "What did I do to you today to deserve that?" As angry as she became with him, she understood that he was taking out his own pain on her, and she refused to add to it. She just wished he would deal with it in some other way. What had she done to him to deserve it?

Anica regraded her reflection this way and that. She wondered what Joshua saw when he looked at himself in the mirror. He was a cute boy, tall and slender, with the same dark brown hair and eyes they both got from their father, but he paid scant attention to his appearance, and he never smiled. She had loved his laugh when they were little. She could not remember when she had last heard it.

"Ani!" her mother cried, "What are you doing in there?"

"Just brushing my hair, Mom."

She donned her pink terry robe and got to doing just that.

When she emerged, Joshua, in his pajamas and slippers, was padding toward the bathroom under the watchful eye of their mother, who was intent on making sure he was really going to brush his teeth.

"Out of the way, jerk-face!" Joshua grumbled at
her. She stuck her tongue out at him as their mother
started scolding him for his remark. It was the best she
could do. Sometimes she could think of a better retort,
but she was tired, and it wasn't worth the effort. She
was tired of fighting with him at all, but if she did not
put up a fight, it would let the hurt in. It hurt anyway,
but she could not let it show.

Anica put on her pajamas and turned off her light.
Her room was warm and stuffy – when was her father
going to do something about the heat? She pulled her
blanket up only to her waist. She wanted to sleep, but
she was uncomfortable in more ways than one. Unable
to sustain her anger towards her brother, she started to
cry.

Jerk-face. That was Joshua's epithet *du jour*. He
had called her worse, so maybe he, too, was too tired
to think of anything more clever to jab her with.

She knew he hated the things she did that kept them
apart. If only he understood, he might try to find
something to keep himself occupied, too. The more
Anica did, the less she had to think about her life at
home. The more time she spent with her friends, the
less time she had to spend with her family.

She loved her mother, and she still loved her
brother more than he could possibly know. She loved
her father, too. He was so strong and handsome and

confident. She could not understand why he did not love her back. What had she done? What did she do to make him ignore her? She thought she was doing everything right. She worked hard in school. She kept her room clean. She was polite and respectful to grownups. She was all of the things that Joshua wasn't, the things their father berated him for. She could understand why he did not love Joshua, but why did he care so little for her? It hurt. It hurt a lot, and it had hurt for a long time.

Her teacher and her coach lavished her with praise. Her piano teacher said she was her best pupil. Everyone liked her at school. Mom talked to her all the time, and she was affectionate. She had to be doing something right. Yet her father remained so distant, and Joshua – they were so close once, but now it was *jerk-face*.

Anica gave in to her crying, muffling her sobs with her pillow. If Mom could hear her, she would come in to console her, but she knew if she told her why she cried, it would only make her mother feel worse. Mom already cried for Joshua. Her father was cool to Mom, too. What had *she* done to turn him away, she wondered.

If Joshua could hear her crying, it would wound him, and she could not bear the thought of that. His life was already so bleak. Mom cared for him and she tried to make it better for him, but he pushed her away, too. Anica wanted desperately to help her brother, but it seemed to her that he tried harder to keep her out than he did with anyone else.

Josh and Ani

Joshua could not sleep. He had tossed a meaningless insult at his sister, just because such things had become automatic. But as he passed her in the hall, he noticed that her hair was down. She usually kept it tied back, but after her showers, she brushed it out carefully and let it fall past her shoulders. The way it framed her face made her look so pretty. He had seen her this way countless times before, but this time, he *noticed* her.

After bedtime, the image kept popping into his head. He started to think about how lithe and shapely she looked in her leotards, and then he couldn't get that out of his head, either. Kevin was always telling him he was lucky to have such a pretty sister, but for two years now, Joshua had not thought of her as anything other than annoying. Now it annoyed him that he was starting to see her as a girl.

Anica was busy every day after school. She left directly from school to her lessons, so Joshua usually had the house to himself when he got home. The day after he saw her in the hall, he cautiously entered Anica's room. He moved about the room carefully, surveying her possessions. She was scrupulously neat and she would notice if he disturbed anything. There was a prominent shelf above her bed, arrayed with trophies, medals, and ribbons she'd won for gymnastics and piano competitions. On the wall surrounding it were a number of framed certificates, more awards and accolades.

Joshua was envious. He could admit to himself that she deserved every one of them, but all he had on his own wall were some Star Wars posters and the picture of good old Jesus his father had hung. All of it reminded Joshua of what a loser he was. He lost interest in her things and decided to go back to his room to try to think about something other than the pink bathrobe that hung on a hook behind her door.

As he turned to go, he noticed something else. On her nightstand was a picture of him and Anica posing close together, arms around each other, when he was six and she was four. He wondered why she would have it there. Maybe Mom had put it there, he thought, and Anica didn't want to hurt her feelings.

He remembered the picture. Mom had taken them to the mall with her, and on a whim, she took them into the portrait studio there. She bought several prints for the family, including two for him and Anica. Joshua had stashed his somewhere, and when he returned to his room, he started rummaging for it. He found it in the bottom drawer of his dresser, where he kept some of his winter clothes.

He sat down at his cluttered desk to study it. He and his sister were holding one another closely. *Ani was so cute then,* Joshua thought. He remembered them posing for the picture. Their embrace was spontaneous, and the photographer didn't need to position them against the backdrop. He'd only had to get them to smile at the camera instead of each other.

He did not return the picture to his dresser drawer. He placed it on his desk, behind the mountain of clutter he had there, knowing Anica hated being in his room and she would not see it.

His mom picked Anica up from her lessons on her way home from work. Today was Thursday, and that meant gymnastics. They got in the door around 6:00 PM, bundled up against the cold December air. Anica removed her coat to reveal that she was still in her leotard, having put on just a pair of sweatpants before she left practice. He had seen her in her leos before, but seeing her that way now startled him. *Damn it, Kevin. You're right, she is a pretty girl. She gets prettier every day, and she has to be my sister!*

Anica went upstairs to change her clothes. Joshua waited a few minutes and followed her. He stood in the hallway outside of her room, listening to her movements inside. A couple of drawers opened and closed. Some coathangers scraped across the rod in her closet. He heard her unzip her backpack and the sound of papers shuffling, the creak of the back of her desk chair.

Joshua retreated to his room and opened his own backpack. He pulled out his math folder and took out the worksheet he'd pretended to start in study hall. Reading the first problem and looking at the nonsense he'd scrawled under it, he downheartedly stuffed it back into his backpack and laid down on his bed to close his eyes. He hadn't slept well the night before, and he dozed off until his mother called up the stairs that it was time for dinner. Dinner with his father!

Joshua's father owned an insurance agency. He was usually gone until late in the evening calling and visiting clients, but a day or two a week, and every Friday, he left his office to come home for dinner. Joshua knew his father would get home at 6:30 on the dot and would expect the table to be set and everyone to be seated. It was almost 6:30 now, so he hurriedly scurried down the stairs. He barely had time to tuck in his shirt and sit down at the kitchen table before he heard the garage door open and his father's car pulling in.

Anica was now dressed in loose corduroy overalls and a yellow T-shirt. She'd have been hard pressed to find anything less provocative to wear, but Joshua still felt something different when taking his seat across the table from her. Once again, her hair was down and beautifully brushed. He liked the way it caught the light, shimmering when she turned her head. Everything about her seemed softer. He studied her delicate hands and her wrists. He'd paid scant attention to them before, but he thought they were pretty, too, just like her face and her hair.

He looked away from his sister when his father stepped in from the garage. John Miller wordlessly surveyed the table that was set before him, his wife and children seated stiffly in their places. Then he took off his shoes and left momentarily to put his overcoat in the closet. When he returned, he sat at the head of the table and his family dutifully bowed their heads for grace.

Joshua nearly forgot it was his turn to say the words, and it took a not-so-gentle kick under the table from his sister to jar him into attentiveness.

"H-heavenly Father, we, we thank thee for the gifts we are about to receive in Jesus's name, Amen."

All throughout the meal, Joshua tried to keep his eyes and his mind off his sister, but it was impossible. Just seeing her in her leotard had upset his applecart. Seeing her now with her beautiful hair down upset it even more. After bedtime, he did not even try to push Anica out of his head. It surprised him that he didn't even want to.

Friday morning began as every other schoolday morning did, with Joshua languishing in bed as everyone else was getting dressed for breakfast. He groggily sat up when his mother came in to nag him. He put on the pants he had worn yesterday and the first shirt he could find in his closet, made his way downstairs, and entered the kitchen for breakfast.

Anica sat at the table while Mom prepared breakfast. Dad got up and left the house for work early each day, which was a relief.

As he picked at his scrambled eggs, he regarded Anica sitting across the table from him. She was wearing a black velvet jumper over a prim white blouse that was buttoned up to her neck. Her silky brown hair was pulled back into a ponytail that hung to the center of her back. Her big, brown eyes and long lashes held him even as she looked up from her plate to glare at him. Her eyes, so beautiful, from the time she was little. He'd been squabbling with her for so long he'd forgotten, but now...

"What are you looking at?" Anica snapped at him, shattering his reverie.

"J-just your face," was all he could say. His voice was defensive but not angry.

"What's wrong with it?" She asked him, still irritated, but more softly.

"Nothing. Sorry."

Anica gave him a puzzled look, then went back to her breakfast.

Mom told them both to get their coats on before they were late for school. Anica walked to Lincolncrest Elementary School with Jessica and Joanna, while Joshua walked the nine blocks to Truman Junior High alone. His mood deteriorated with each footstep as he contemplated the long day ahead of

64

him. Nevertheless, he walked more quickly, even jogged a little bit, so as to ensure he would avoid a tardy slip and the after school detention that came with it. He couldn't bear the thought of losing an hour out of his weekend.

On Fridays, school went even slower than usual. His mouth was dry as he handed forward the wreckage of his math homework – sometimes Mrs. Simmons would quickly scan through the homework before she started her lesson, which could mean he'd have to stay after school, but today, she just put it in a folder and started to write some confusing arrangements of numbers on the whiteboard.

Lunch period went by far more quickly, as it did every day. He sat alone at a small table with a wobbly leg, gazing across the cafeteria at Becky Lindstrom. She still didn't know he was alive, but he avoided her whenever he thought she could actually see him. If she ever actually looked at him, she would see what a loser he was. Seeing Becky was the only thing that made him look forward to school, and it broke his heart every day when the 5th period bell rang and she left the cafeteria.

Joshua didn't have any friends to sit with at lunch. He and Kevin still got together, but he missed having a buddy at school. Despite their long friendship, Joshua sometimes thought himself so unlikable he suspected the only reason Kevin still came to his house was his infatuation with Anica. She paid him no mind when he was there, but he would would gaze at her longingly when she wasn't looking. Now I'm doing it, Joshua thought dismayingly.

Joshua's last period was a study hall for kids who didn't do well in school, losers like himself who would avoid one another lest their loserdom should become cemented for all time. The teacher would occasionally stroll about the room, checking to see who was and wasn't working. Joshua had his math workbook open to the assigned page and he busied himself by copying each incomprehensible problem onto a separate sheet of paper. He would scrawl something containing some of the numbers from the problem in the space below, hoping old Mrs. Addison wouldn't stop to scrutinize his work. That could mean staying after school, too. When she wasn't looking, his eyes were on the wall clock, which seemed to take forever to tick away each minute.

At last, the bell rang. Joshua wanted to bolt from his seat, but Mrs. Addison insisted on making the kids line up to exit the room one by one. When he finally escaped, he made his way quickly to his locker, sloppily crammed his homework into his backpack, and headed for the south door, free at last.

On passing the north side of the building, he looked around nervously for Jesse Duncan. To his relief, he was nowhere in sight. He also watched the pickup lane, hoping to see Mrs. Lindstrom's Mercedes and a chance to get a last look at Becky. She was nowhere in sight, either, so he pulled the hood of his jacket over his head and started off for home.

Joshua reclined on his bed after he got home. Anica. What had she done to him? This was not some inaccessible girl from his school. She lived in this house with him, and the thought of her long, shiny hair kept coming into his head, and the way she looked from the side when her mouth was open a little. The jumper she wore this morning was pretty on her, even if he couldn't see anything that might excite him.

He thought of the picture of him and her on Anica's nightstand. He went to his desk and moved his to his own nightstand. Mom might see it, but Anica still never entered his messy room.

I'm in love with my own sister, Joshua thought. What else could explain how he felt?

He heard the garage door open. Mom and Ani! He wanted to be there when his sister walked in the door, so he grabbed a book from his backpack and hurried down the stairs. He flopped onto the sofa with it just as his mother entered, carrying two bags of groceries.

"Josh, help your sister with the groceries, please!"

Joshua would normally have voiced a complaint about how he was too busy, but he hopped off the sofa with a quick "Okay, Mom."

He hurried into the garage where Anica was busy

67

taking bags out of the trunk. His heart jumped when he saw her face. He lightly touched her hands, each of which held a heavy bag of canned goods.

"Here, Ani, let me get those."

Anica's face twisted into a puzzled frown.

"Why are you being nice to me?" She demanded. "Did you break something of mine?"

"Er, I-i'm just hungry" he blurted out lamely.

"There'd better be nothing missing from my room!" she said, reaching for some of the other bags that remained in her mother's trunk. When they finished unloading the car, Anica turned to him and muttered,

"Thanks, Josh." She was not enthusiastic, but she was sincere. She never said those words to him now except when she was being sarcastic.

That's new, Joshua puzzled to himself. So many feelings. Anxiety. Bewilderment. Wonder. Desire.

Love.

It was Friday evening. That meant no homework and staying up later before bed. Dad went upstairs to work. The rest of the family gathered around the TV to watch a movie. Joshua sat on the sofa next to his sister. He turned his head to regard her face, so lovely in profile. When he moved a little closer to her, she turned her head to him and said,

"Josh, What are you looking at? What's gotten into you?" Her face was puzzled. Her voice was inquisitive but not angry.

68

"You, uh, have a little spaghetti sauce on your chin." Joshua reached for a Kleenex and made to wipe the imaginary spot off, but she snatched it from him and said,

"Where?"

"Uh, it's gone. I think it must have been just a crumb."

With a frown, Anica wadded up the Kleenex and set it in her lap, but she did not move away from Joshua. Her hand, so pretty, so close – he longed to take it into his. What in the hell was he going to do about this? He was saddened, yet relieved, when the movie was over and she padded off to her room.

When bedtime arrived, Joshua's contorted emotions tossed him around like a leaf in the wind. Tonight, on passing her in the hall on the way to the bathroom, Joshua could not think of something nasty to say. He did not want to. He said only "Goodnight, Ani" in an uncharacteristically sincere voice. He braced himself for something snarky, but she just turned her head and said,

"Goodnight, Josh," with something that might have been the beginnings of a smile.

Joshua brushed his teeth and returned to his room. Long after the house was settled, he was wide awake, unable to get her out of his mind. A terrible, provocative thought entered his head. He tried to dispel it, but he could not. Hours passed. He was still unable to sleep, his mind on his sister sleeping just down the hall.

The clock on Joshua's nightstand read 2:17. He couldn't fight it any longer. Joshua kept a small flashlight near his bed. He switched it on, pointing it at the ceiling. The light was dim, but he could see well enough.

What are we doing? his internal voice was shouting at him. *What if she wakes up? What if she screams? Mom and Dad...*

It was still shouting at him, but the pounding in his chest was drowning it out as he noiselessly turned the latch on his door and stepped out into the hallway. It was illuminated by a dim night light and another, similar night light shining through the open door of the bathroom. No light came from the gap under the door to his parents' room and the house was dead quiet.

The dread inside of him grew greater with each step away from the safety of his room, yet he moved, silently, slowly, deliberately, toward Anica's door. He paused there to listen intently once again for any signs of stirring anywhere in the house and especially from within her room. His heart was thudding rapidly, yet he kept his breathing slow and controlled. He carefully gripped Anica's doorknob. It turned silently and smoothly and in a moment it was open. In another moment, he was inside and silently closing the door behind him. He did not know what he was going to do in there, but he had to see her.

The room was stuffy. Joshua pointed his flashlight at the ceiling and turned it on. Anica was sound asleep, breathing very slowly and regularly. She lay on her back with one arm above her head. Her bedclothes covered her only to the waist. He moved closer to her bed and knelt there, aiming the flashlight at the near wall so to as better illuminate her without shining it into her eyes. Anica's cotton print pajamas were as modest as everything else she wore, but she made everything she wore look pretty. As she slept, he gazed at her, studying every nuance. The hand she held above her pillow was palm up, her fingers relaxed and curled inward. Her nails were neatly pared. It reminded Joshua of a flower unfolding, delicate and beautiful.

Joshua's eyes turned to her face. Her long lashes were even prettier when her eyes were closed. Her lips were slightly parted, her perfect white teeth visible. She was beautiful, so beautiful, so innocent, and so vulnerable. A powerful wave of shame suddenly washed over him. What was he doing? He adored her! How could he take advantage of her this way? He rose from her bedside and quietly retreated to his own room. The wave of shame became a deluge. He had stolen something from her, and he had abused her. He had been abusing her since the fourth grade, tearing her down whenever someone else had done the same

71

to him. She didn't ask for it, just as she did not invite him to come into her room and look at something she had a right to keep to herself.

Joshua began to cry. Tears of remorse, tears of despair, tears of grief, tears of loneliness. He took the picture of Anica and him from his nightstand and held it to his heart. In the dim light of the flashlight he'd used to invade her room, he looked at her face, next to his own. She was smiling and holding him tight.

Ani, Ani, I'm sorry. How could I do this to you? Why did I do this to you? You didn't deserve it. I don't deserve you. Ani, I love you so much, and I miss you.

Joshua cried himself to sleep, still clutching the photograph in his hand. His last thoughts were of how beautiful she had looked as she slept, a vision he had stolen, an act he could never take back.

Agnes

Agnes Miller methodically made her way down the hall, emptying wastebaskets, picking up clutter, dusting the furniture, and cleaning the mirrors. She always cleaned on Saturday since she worked all week and her husband kept a rule about abstaining from work on Sundays. Anica's room was a joy to behold - everything in its place, bed made, dirty clothes in the hamper. She needed to do little more than dust lightly and empty the wastebasket. Not five minutes in and out.

Then there was Joshua's room. This chore would take her more time than the rest of the upstairs put together. His floor was littered with toys, dirty clothes, half-eaten food, and some things she couldn't identify. Her broken Mixmaster egg beater lay half-disassembled on the floor next to his cluttered desk. His bed was an unmade riot, his mirrors were streaked, and she had to move or put away dozens of things before she could dust. She sighed and got to work.

Joshua's wastebasket was overflowing. She would have to empty it into the large garbage bag she had in tow before she could start, and there would be enough trash scattered about the room to fill it again at least once. There were several wads of paper towels in it, and more under his bed where he kept his roll of fresh ones. There were more of them this week than usual.

Agnes chuckled. *Some girl really has him going*, she thought. She amused herself with the idea that she should get him another wastebasket just for this, though it would embarrass him to death.

It had been months, she lamented. His twelfth birthday had come and gone. When was John going to have the talk with him? Ever? Because of his religious beliefs, he had opted him out of fifth grade sex education, and she could hardly tell him herself. She had been counseling Anica about it since she was eight, but poor Joshua! He seemed to be figuring some of it out on his own, but there was so much he had to know. Even before he entered puberty, she told him about how he should treat girls, how he should respect them and listen to them, but she could not tell him most of the things he needed to know now.

After her children had gone to bed, she retired for the night. John was already asleep. She frowned at her husband, snoring and sputtering on his side of their big king bed. He hadn't touched her since she was pregnant with Anica. It made her sad and not a little angry. She had never lost the twenty pounds she'd put on having Joshua, and she'd put on another twenty with her daughter. That pregnancy had been very difficult, culminating in an emergency C section, and it left her unable to conceive any more children. The doctors told her she should consider a hysterectomy. She wanted no part of that. She had an infant and a toddler to care for after her difficult recovery, and little help at home.

After Anica was born, her husband lost interest in her. Yet she was still a flesh and blood woman, she thought bitterly. Sometimes she blamed herself, but what else could she have done? She nearly lost her daughter in childbirth. Caring for her and Joshua was exhausting. Was she really supposed to pay more attention to her appearance? Or was she supposed to pay more attention to him?

She was more concerned about how he treated the children. He had virtually ignored Anica since she was a tiny infant in an incubator. Anica would not speak of it, but Agnes knew it hurt her terribly. Agnes loved her children equally, she thought, but little Ani was so sensitive. She would break into tears at the sight of a dead sparrow. She wanted to fill the chasm her father left in her life, but she knew she could not.

Agnes so much wanted to shelter her from the ugly things in the world. Ani was guileless and vulnerable. She was also very smart, which gave Agnes some comfort, but was she smart enough to know if she were being manipulated? Anica was a beautiful child. She would grow more beautiful as she progressed through adolescence. Agnes worried that someone would take advantage of her innocence and the way she yearned for a father's love. An older boy, perhaps, or worse, a coach or some other grownup in a position of authority or trust. The thought terrified her, so she gave her more attention than she gave her son, keeping her trust so she would talk to her about her life.

Thinking of Joshua often brought her tears. Her firstborn needed so much that she could not give him. John devoted most of his attention to his work and his church. When he was home, what little time he spent with Joshua was in tearing him down for his grades, or his forgetfulness, or his sloppy living habits. Never once had he taken him out into the yard to play catch, or took him fishing, or anything else a loving father might do with his son.

Agnes had spoken to her husband many times about both of their children. When she spoke to him about Anica, he told her he didn't know anything about girls. His own father did not let him socialize with girls when he was a boy, and his mother was a timid soul who practically worshiped the man. Agnes had grown up with two sisters, he explained, so the job of raising their daughter was best left to her.

How could he not love her, though? Or if he did, how could he not show it? She was sweet and adorable. She just wanted to be acknowledged. Was it so hard for him to show her a little affection? Even an occasional smile would mean the world to Anica.

When she protested his treatment of their son, his response was that it was a hard, cold world out there, and he needed to be hard on him to teach him how to survive. John had been on his own since he was sixteen, and everything he had in this world he fought for on his own terms. Did it ever occur to him that it didn't have to be that way for his son? This was not rural Tennessee and they were not poor.

John worked hard to provide for them. They had a nice house in a good neighborhood. They had food on the table and clothes on their backs. They could go to the doctor when they were sick. He had established college funds for both of their children when they were born. From John's point of view, he did more than enough for his wife and children. It seemed futile for her to explain to him that his children both needed his love and approval. From what Agnes knew of John's childhood, his father had given him neither.

Agnes thought fondly of her own father. Like John, he was a self-made man, who had worked his way up from being a hod carrier to owning a large, successful construction company. Like John, he married later in life, and like John, he worked long hours to keep his business thriving. Unlike John, he made up for it by lavishing attention on his five children whenever he could be with them. She once sat on his shoulders to watch a parade. He dressed up as a pirate and took his children trick-or-treating. He decorated the Christmas tree with them.

When Agnes was thirteen, he sold his company for a sizable fortune so he could spend more time with his family. Less than two years later, he died of lymphoma. The memory always saddened Agnes. Her father was gone many years before Joshua was born. Had he only survived, he might have been the presence in Joshua's life that he needed.

Agnes desperately missed his presence in her own life. Whenever she felt afraid and insecure as a child, she could take comfort in his strength and guidance. She shared her daughter's sensitivity and her son's self-doubt. She had felt herself adrift after her father died. They were exceptionally close, as she was born much later than her older siblings, and she was the apple of his eye; he was her rock, her compass.

When John came along, he was so strong, so smart, so confident. She still relied on these things in him, even when she disagreed with him. If only her children could see these things in him. If only her son could look beyond his fear of his father, perhaps he could learn something from his example. But perhaps he was learning something. John, like their son, seemed so distant and withdrawn now. He was seldom home before the children were asleep, and he left the house before they were awake.

Her brother Alan lived only half an hour away. He doted on Joshua and Anica, and they both looked up to him, but he had five young children of his own, and he was too busy with his own brood to provide her children with the kind of attention they needed. Her older brother lived in Texas and they only saw him around the holidays.

There were no other men in Joshua's life to show him how to be a man. His male teachers scolded him. The pastor at John's church was a sanctimonious ass. Joshua never went out for sports, and he didn't even like watching them. There was no coach he could look up to. There weren't even any baseball or football stars he could look to for inspiration.

The boy was smart, very smart. The psychologist from his school had said so, but John had stood in the way when she said he also needed help. John thought he needed only discipline to straighten him out, and he thought Agnes was far too soft on him. He thought that ADHD and dyslexia were shams cooked up by the big drug companies to make money.

Joshua loathed school, for good reason. His teachers berated him. Other children laughed at him or bullied him if they paid any attention at all. His one good friend moved out of the neighborhood the summer before he started middle school. He had no other friends that Agnes knew of.

Agnes made a half-hearted effort at making him do his homework, but she saw how frustrated he became when he tried to do it. He refused her efforts to help him – out of pride or embarrassment; she did not know. She wanted to get him a tutor, but John, once again, would have none of it. All the boy needed was to apply himself, he told her.

"Oh, for the love of God, Agnes," he'd said recently, "just look at his room! He's lazy! How is a tutor going to fix that?" John insisted. "Just more money down the drain. Sometimes, I'm ashamed I have to give that boy a roof over his head!"

Joshua spent a lot of time playing alone in his room, and she seldom heard him laugh or even saw him smile. He bickered with his sister constantly, only in part because of the attention Agnes gave her. Anica was talented musically and athletically, and she worked diligently to develop her gifts. Joshua had a great deal of aptitude for many things, but he was easily frustrated and seldom completed anything he started.

Agnes wondered if things could have been different. Joshua wanted nothing to do with preschool because it would mean time away from Ani. If he'd been made to go, would it have helped? Maybe his problems would have been discovered earlier, but John would likely have been as opposed to getting him help as he was now. And his connection to his sister was so strong. Would it have been better for either of them had she separated them earlier? The bond between them was so strong, Agnes believed, that they could not go on bickering forever.

Joshua was quiet, often stammering when he did speak, and he was terribly shy. Ani was warm and outgoing, well liked by everyone, and she was disarmingly pretty. Joshua had once confessed to Agnes that he thought he was ugly, even though the one good thing his father had given him were his good looks.

In spite of how badly he was treated, Joshua was a good boy who never acted out or talked back. This was not for fear of punishment, it was just how he was. Agnes took some pride in this, but in truth, she sometimes wished he were more rebellious, just to see him stand up for himself. When John came down on him, he would bow his head, nodding and mumbling apologies occasionally, and wait until it was over. Agnes often thought she should intervene, but it would anger her husband if he believed she was trying to undermine his authority.

Ironically, John was bitter about his own mother having stood by wordlessly while his father unleashed his wrath on him. This was different, Agnes told herself; John believed he was doing right by the boy in treating him the way he did. She had never seen him punish Joshua any more severely than sending him to his room. Although John never spoke of it, she knew his own father had done far worse.

Her son needed love, understanding, and guidance. She tried to give him those things, but he was shut off. Joshua was respectful of her, and she knew that he loved her, but whenever she tried to get close to him, he withdrew. He could not talk to her about the things that were hurting him, and it was clear that he was hurting. She cried for him, but she did not know how to reach him.

Agnes entered the master bath to draw herself a tub. Perhaps a relaxing bath could soothe her troubled mind. She looked at herself unhappily in the mirror as she disrobed. She had let herself go after Anica was born, and now she was getting lines in her face.

John just seemed to get better looking as he aged. He was forty-nine now, gray at the temples, but the lines in his face just gave him character. His stomach was flat and his muscles were hard. Agnes still enjoyed looking at him despite their problems. He was so charming and handsome when they met that he swept her off her feet. She remembered how they had once been so much in love.

Agnes and John

Agnes Adler was happy the day was coming to a close. She was a pretty woman with hazel eyes and sandy blond hair. She worked at the Davis-Adler Construction Company, meeting with realtors and prospective buyers to show the new properties her company built. Business was good. They had six new housing developments under construction, along with two office buildings and an upscale townhome complex.

Today was Friday. Friday afternoons were always slow, and Agnes liked her job a lot more when she had something to do. She had not shown a property since 11:00 AM. She was starting to pack up for the day when a man entered the office, carrying a brochure from the townhomes the company was building. He was a tall man, physically fit, well groomed, and impeccably dressed in a well-tailored charcoal gray suit. Agnes guessed he would be in his middle thirties. He had rich brown hair and striking dark eyes. He wore a nice wristwatch, but he wore no rings. In his lapel, he wore a small gold cross. Agnes could not remember when she last saw such a good looking man.

"Excuse me, ma'am, I've been looking at these properties, and your brochure said I should ask about them here. This looks to be just about what I'm in the market for."

He spoke in a rich baritone with a tempered Southern accent. His manner fit his grooming.

"Name's Miller, John Miller. These condos have been going up across the street from the office park where I have my business. Good materials, and your men are taking their time. Impressive."

John offered his hand. His grip was gentle and his hand was warm. His nails were nicely manicured and his smile was radiant.

"Pleased to meet you, Mr. Miller. I'm Agnes, Agnes Adler. The models are open, but the first units won't be available until fall. You can reserve a unit with a deposit. Would you like a tour? I could show you the models tonight." Agnes might have sent anyone else home and asked them to come back later, but she wanted to spend some time with this beautiful man.

"That would be gracious of you. I know it's late in the day, but I don't get much time. My business takes most of it."

"I don't mind in the least, Mr. Miller. It's my job. I just need to close the office before we go."

Agnes checked the doors and windows, turned off the lights, and set the alarm. They left the building together. Agnes began walking towards her Toyota Camry.

"Ma'am, if you don't mind, could we take my car? I need the legroom." John gestured to a big Ford

Explorer parked near the building

"It's Agnes, please. And it's not a problem at all."

John opened the door of his car for Agnes before getting in to drive. A gentleman, too, Agnes thought. She had known John Miller for five minutes, but she was already taken with him. She supposed he was married, although he did not wear a wedding band. As they left the parking lot, He gestured to the sign in front of the building.

"Family business, ma'am? I'm sorry, Agnes. You told me your name was Adler."

"Yes, it is. My father used to own it, this half of it anyway. He sold it to Davis Construction twelve years ago. I just work here, really, but we are like a family. The owner was Dad's best friend. He came to our house all the time when I was growing up. They started out together working construction. Dad was a hod carrier, Uncle Mike – Mr. Davis – was a carpenter. They each saved up their money and started their own businesses. They became rivals, but it didn't affect their friendship. They used to bet one another a case of beer when they competed for a contract. The competition was good for both of them. They drank a lot of beer, and they built a lot of houses."

"Your father is a man after my own heart, ma'am – there I go again, Agnes, I'm sorry. And you can call me John. You know, I started out as a construction worker myself. When I moved here from Tennessee,

85

there was a recession on, and there weren't a lot of companies hiring. I got a job working for a man who owned an insurance agency. Just odd jobs at first, but after I'd worked there for a while, he convinced me to study for an insurance license. That was a lot of work, but Vince – my boss – somehow knew it would suit me. I took over the agency when he retired.

"Your father must have retired in style," John continued, "Big outfit, I see your projects everywhere."

"It was never about the money for him," Agnes told him. "He took enough of the profits to give us a good home, but he put most of it back into his business. When Uncle Mike finally convinced Dad to sell the company to him, he came away with a lot of money. I'm sorry, Mr. Miller – John, I don't mean to boast, but I'm proud of my father. I just wish he'd lived longer. He got cancer and died just a couple of years after he sold his company."

"I'm sorry to hear that," John said sincerely. "He left you money, but you still work in an office?"

"Oh, yes. Before he died, my dad put it all in a living trust that my mother controls. Dad invested well, and it's worth twice what it was when he set it up. Mom and Dad both didn't want to act like rich people. We lived in the same house they bought when they married. When all of us were grown and out of the house, she sold it and bought a little three bedroom

86

ranch in Oak Hills. She's had her car for ten years.

"We got money for our educations, but that was it. He wanted his children to learn how to work for a living before they would come into money. We divide the trust when my mother passes, but we aren't in any hurry. My sisters, my older brother and I went to college and got good jobs. My younger brother enlisted in the Army. He's fighting in Afghanistan now."

"Your father is a man after my own heart. I like a man who knows value of a good day's work. I can see why you're proud of him."

"How did you get your education?" Agnes asked. "You told me there was a lot of study involved to get into your line of work."

John laughed a little.

"Ah, a little of this, a little of that. A lot of hard knocks. I mostly did a lot of reading. When I was growing up in Tennessee, I read everything I could get my hands on. Of course, I had to pass some exams to get my insurance license. Vince taught me a thing or two, but most of that was a lot of reading, too. I guess I'm something of a bookworm," John chuckled. "I need a bigger place just to keep all the books I've got."

They had reached the townhome development. Agnes gave John a tour of the models. John said he liked the smallest model because he lived by himself. Agnes was surprised that some girl hadn't snatched him up long ago. She was also surprised at how much this pleased her.

They left the development and John took her back to her car. Before she reached for her shoulder belt, he asked her,

"Agnes, I suspect this has been a long day for both of us. I'm getting hungry. There's a good steak and seafood joint over on Sycamore. I would be most honored if you could join me."

Agnes felt giddy and nervous. Even though she was quite attractive, she had not dated much since she left college. She did not, however, hesitate. This man had stepped out of her dreams.

"I would be most honored to join you for dinner, John Miller!"

The restaurant was crowded when they arrived. People were waiting at the entrance to get a table, but a server approached and smiled at them when they walked in.

"It's nice to see you with company for a change, Mr. Miller. Right this way."

The server seated them at a small table in a corner. She brought them water and menus and asked them what they would like to drink.

"Just water, as usual, Dorothy."

Agnes wanted a glass of wine, but she did now know how John felt about alcohol. She ordered an iced tea instead. She wondered how they had gotten a table right away. Sensing her thoughts, John told her,

"The owner is a client of mine. We go back. I eat here on Fridays, so they keep a table open for me."

"What products do you sell, John? Uncle Mike is always looking for a break on the insurance."

"Just life insurance, but we do offer group term insurance if your boss would be interested. I'd advise you that our premiums are a bit higher than market because we donate a portion of each premium to Christian charities around the world. Tax deductible, of course. We sell mostly to people of faith."

"I noticed the cross you wear," Agnes remarked.

"I'm a Christian, Agnes. That's important to me. This cross, it's a symbol of resurrection and life." John smiled. "You'll see these all over town, too. Do you go to church on Sundays?"

Agnes was a little crestfallen. It did not matter to her that John was religious, but she thought it might matter to him that she was not.

"I was raised Catholic. We went to Mass regularly before Dad died. I'm sorry to say I haven't gone in some time. I was so upset when my father died, and the priest's words sounded so hollow. I guess I lost my faith."

John reached across the table for her hand. Laying his on top of hers, he gently spoke to her,

"Agnes, people who think they've lost their faith didn't have much to begin with. Now, my pappy told me that Catholics were idolaters, that it went against the Third Commandment. He was a lot more hidebound than I am, old school Pentecostal. I'm a Baptist now, but I don't think it matters very much what church you worship in. The problem is that people go to church and expect to get their religion preached to them.

"Now, I'll bet that priest of yours picked something out of the Bible to say at your father's funeral. And I'll bet those words didn't have much meaning for you. Do you have a Bible at home?"

Agnes felt smaller by the minute, but John had not removed his hand.

"I think my mother has one somewhere," she said meekly.

"I keep one at home, and I keep one in my office. I read some from it every day. Agnes, faith doesn't come from being ministered to, and it doesn't come from sacraments or confessing every little sin to a man behind a screen. You have to work at it, but in my estimation, it's worth the effort. You said your brother is fighting in Afghanistan. I'll bet you worry for him."

In spite of herself, Agnes started to sob. John held her hand more tightly.

"Every day. I worry for him every day, and sometimes it keeps me up at night. He sends me letters every week. He's a sergeant now, he just started his second deployment. I'm so proud of him, but I'm so afraid. Why did he have to go back?"

"You're right to be proud of him. Your brother's a good man, a brave man, Agnes. He's on the side of righteousness, fighting some very bad people. The worst kind of people, those Taliban – they perverted their faith to use as a weapon. Even the Book they claim to read is against everything they do.

"God doesn't want any part of that. It's all in the Bible. Now I know people have attitudes, they call people like me Bible thumpers or worse. But when I look at this world, it's clear as day what the Scriptures are trying to tell us. If people would just heed the words of the Lord, then your brother would be home right now. There wouldn't be a war going on anywhere. Isaiah 2:4, it's right there in black and white for everyone to see."

He had her there, Agnes admitted to herself. She still worried that she had alienated the charming, handsome, and intelligent man sitting across from her.

"None of it's your fault, Agnes. There're a lot more people in this world who've lost their way than those who've found it. Anybody can see you're a good woman. I don't care about when you last went to church. There're people who go to church every Sunday, and the rest of the time, they're in sin up to their eyeballs."

John removed his hand and smiled broadly at her.

"So tell me more about your father, Agnes. I like

91

him. The people I like always have stories to go with them, and I'll bet you have a few to tell."

Agnes told John more about her family. She was the fourth of five children. Her older brother and her sisters were born close together, but five more years passed before Agnes was born. Her younger brother followed close behind her, and they became very close.

Her older brother Aaron lived in Houston, Texas. Her two older sisters, Adele and Alice, lived nearby. She thought it was funny that her parents gave all of them names that started with 'A,' but her father had told them it would get them to the top of any list they'd be on.

Aaron was an engineer with a technology company. Adele and Alice both went into nursing. Agnes herself had majored in marketing, which prepared her for the job she held. Uncle Mike confessed that he'd given it to her partly out of nepotism – but it would be up to Agnes to keep it.

Her younger brother Alan was a serious, principled young man. Twelve years separated him from Aaron, and as the youngest, Agnes thought, perhaps he thought he had that much more to prove. Despite all of their objections, he left college and joined the Army after 9/11. She was both mad at him and proud of him, but after listening to what John said about him, she was a little less mad and a little more proud. She just wished she was less worried.

"What about you, John. Tell me about your family."

John's face grew somber.

"I grew up in a little place called Arlo, Tennessee. Only around a thousand people in the whole town. There wasn't much there. I was sixteen when my pappy died. My momma moved back in with her folks. There wasn't anything for me there, so I left. Not much of a story, really."

Agnes did not want to press him for details. It was clear to her the subject was uncomfortable for him. John grew more animated and talkative when he spoke about his life as a young man in Chicago. The man who hired him for his first job there became his mentor and his friend. He spoke fondly of him, as if he had become a second father. He was in poor health when he retired and only lived a few more years before he passed.

They talked well into the evening. The crowd in the restaurant had thinned out considerably by the time they left and John drove Agnes back to her car again.

"Agnes," John told her, "I very much enjoyed your company tonight. I work too much and it gets lonely. I would like to see you again."

"I'd like that too, John. I'm free tomorrow."

Agnes did not want to appear to be throwing herself at him, but she was giddy and excited. John got out of the car and opened her door for her. He walked her over to her car. Before she reached into her purse for her keys, he held her gently and kissed her. She kissed him back.

"Tomorrow it is," he told her. "7:00, and wear a nice dress."

Today was the happiest day of Agnes's life. Last night at dinner, John took a small velvet box from his pocket and opened it to reveal a two carat diamond engagement ring. In front of everyone at the restaurant where they had their first date, he dropped to one knee and proposed. Tears of joy flooded Agnes's eyes, and she immediately said yes. The people in the restaurant clapped and cheered.

They had been seeing one another for six months. John bought one of the condominiums her company built. He took her there often, and she loved being with him. They had kissed, passionately at times, but he never tried to go farther than that. Agnes supposed his religion prohibited premarital sex, so she respected the choices he made. He was demonstrative enough for her to know how he felt.

She had told him she had been with other men, not many, and only with men she was in a relationship with. This did not seem to bother him at all. She loved this about him, that he could be so committed to his faith, yet he was so understanding of how other people

94

lived.

Today was a Saturday. John told her he had to work most Saturdays because that was when he could meet with a lot of his clients. If there was anything Agnes did not like about John, it was his commitment to his business. She remembered that her father had been the same way, so she understood.

He picked her up at 6:00. They had dinner and went to John's place afterward. Agnes sat down on the sofa. She held her hand out to study her ring.

"It's so beautiful, John. I just can't get over it."

John regarded her with a gleam in his eye. He sat on the sofa with her and put his arms around her.

"The most beautiful thing in this room is you!"

He began to kiss her and she eagerly returned his affection. It became more and more passionate. John began to unbutton her blouse. Agnes grew very aroused and stroked his chest while he finished. She slipped out of it and cast it aside. He put his hand on her breast and returned to his kissing. Agnes reached for the buttons of his shirt and started to undo them.

John paused to deal with his shirt. He grasped it by its placket and ripped it apart, scattering the buttons everywhere. His chest was magnificent. His pectorals were beautifully defined, and his stomach was flat and ripped. He had a generous amount of hair that Agnes found sensual and exciting. His arms and shoulders were muscular, but not musclebound. The sight of him now was overwhelming.

Agnes did not think about why this change would suddenly come over John, but she had long been eager for it. She reached behind herself to unhook her bra, and she cast it aside on the back of the sofa. John picked her up as if she were as light as a feather and carried her into the bedroom. She peeled off her slacks and underwear in a single movement and unbuckled his belt. In a moment, he was naked and all the more breathtaking. The sinews of his thighs were as defined as his chest and his arms, and his legs were also covered in rich dark hair.

He took her like a ravenous beast. She surrendered to him and climaxed harder than she knew was possible. When it was finally over, she knew this was how it was supposed to be between a man and a woman so in love. Her life with him would be incredible.

John lay on his back, recovering his breath. Agnes put her head on his chest, and he put his arm around her to hold her close.

"I love you, Agnes," John proclaimed. "Let's get married. Let's get married tomorrow!"

Agnes was astonished that he would say such a thing, but the idea thrilled her. What would a big church wedding be like, anyway? She came from a big family. John had no family to speak of. There was no one to walk her down the aisle, no one to give her away, and who would say the words? Her family would want a Catholic wedding. She had been attending church with John, but she did not like the minister there. Yes, just elope! Nothing else made more sense.

She spent the night with him in his bed, making love again. In the morning, John drove her to the airport and bought two first class tickets to Las Vegas. John rented a car at the airport there and drove to the first wedding chapel they could find. On February 24th, 2003, John Miller and Agnes Adler were pronounced man and wife.

They found a room at a good hotel away from the Strip. John eschewed gambling and did not care to take in the floor shows and the other sinful recreations the city had to offer. Agnes was perfectly happy with this, because it meant more time alone with John – with her husband! They stayed there only one night, making the best of their wedding night, and the following morning, they were on a plane headed home.

John promised her they would plan a better honeymoon. Agnes was pleased with the idea, but she had what she wanted. When they got home to Glen Park, they stopped at Agnes's small apartment to pick up some of her things and went back to John's townhouse. He carried her over the threshold and straight into the bedroom.

They would remain there for the rest of the day and into the next morning, making only short trips to the refrigerator and the bathroom. Agnes watched John as he rose from their bed. He was as magnificent from behind as he was from the front, but she could not help but notice a number of old, faded scars covering his buttocks and the backs of his legs. When he returned, she gently ran her hands over the slight ridges she felt on his buttocks.

"How did you get these?" She asked.

John's expression became grave. He sat on the edge of the bed, facing away from her for a moment. Agnes was alarmed, but then he turned to her and smiled.

"I told you there were some hard knocks," he said. "Now, weren't we going to do something just now?"

Agnes knew he was evading her, but she was too happy to pursue it any farther. They continued making love, and that night, she slept close to him, happier and more content than she could ever remember.

John's condominium was enough for the two of them, but they wanted to start a family, a big one. After a few months together, they bought a lovely, four-bedroom house on a shady street in Glen Park, in a neighborhood where the houses were nice, but not ostentatious.

They seldom argued. John continued to be gracious, the perfect gentleman he was when Agnes met him. His work still demanded more of his time than Agnes liked, but she went into that with eyes open. He made it up to her. He told her she could furnish the house any way she liked. He surprised her with weekend getaways. Agnes could not imagine being happier with any other man, and she loved him more every day.

Their first Christmas together approached. They decorated the house with lights and wreaths, and they went to a place where they could cut their own Christmas tree. Agnes wanted to have Christmas dinner at their new house. Her mother and sisters would be there, and she had invited Aaron and his wife to fly up from Houston with their two children. Alan had been discharged from the Army after being wounded in combat, and this would be his first Christmas with the family in more than three years. John had no family nearby. It seemed a little lopsided to her.

Agnes had not discussed John's family with him in quite some time. She knew there were things he did not want to tell her, but things were different now. They were married and settled, and they had planned on starting a family soon. Agnes decided she should bring up the subject again.

"John, didn't you tell me your mother still lived in Tennessee? I would love to invite her up for the Holidays."

John's mood abruptly darkened.

"Agnes, it's been well nigh twenty years since I

talked to her. I told the last man who asked me about her that there was nothing more for us to talk about."

Agnes touched his face. John grew irritated.

"Agnes, that part of my life was over and done with a long time ago. I told you there was nothing left for me in Arlo when I left, and that meant nothing. Do you understand?"

"John, I'm sorry. I just thought..."

John grew visibly more upset the more she tried to speak with him. Although Agnes was usually deferential to her husband, it was time to clear the air on this.

"John!" she said sharply, "I'm your wife now. I've told you everything, the good things and the bad. I told you things I was afraid you wouldn't like me for. I told you these things because I love you and because I trust you."

Agnes's tone grew less angry, but no less urgent. "Something happened to you there, I know. I know it must have been very painful, and I know you don't want to talk about it. But we can't have secrets from each other, not if we're going to build a life together. Now if you don't want to tell me anything more tonight, then don't tell me, but hear me out. If you have been carrying all that pain around with you for all this time, isn't it time you shared it with somebody? It's me, John. I love you. Nothing you can tell me is going to change that."

100

John's anger drained from him. He moved closer to her and embraced her. He held her hand, and then he told her about his life in Arlo, Tennessee.

Agnes cried for him and held him tightly. That night, they slept very close together. Agnes had brought him to the brink of redemption. If only she could have kept him there.

Cammie

Camryn Yvonne Larsen was delighted to hear from Mrs. Miller. She hadn't been needed for a while, and it would be nice to see the children again. Anica had an important piano recital and they couldn't take Joshua with them because he'd been sick. Agnes, in turn, was delighted that Cammie could come on such short notice. She would have to come right after basketball practice and she wouldn't be able to see her boyfriend later – but the way he'd been treating her, an evening with Joshua Miller sounded like a better date.

She so loved the Miller kids. They were both adorable. She wasn't happy that they hadn't been getting along, but she understood. Everything was so easy for Ani, and she was so easy to love. Poor little Josh struggled so much with school, and it just wasn't his fault that everybody picked on him. Cammie could see why he took it out on his sister, but it was hard for Ani to understand. She felt badly for both of them.

Cammie was an honor student. She'd offered to tutor Joshua at babysitting rates, but Mr. Miller didn't want that. She suspected Joshua didn't want it, either. As much as Cammie adored him, he was not the easiest kid to sit for. His teachers and his father gave him such a hard time, he resented having yet another person telling him what to do. But he was so cute it was easy to forgive him for it.

102

When practice ended, she left Central High in her little Honda Fit and drove straight to the Miller house.

Joshua did not receive the news well.

"B-but Mom! I don't need a babysitter. I'm twelve. I can be here by myself!"

Joshua's mother replied in a gentle voice. "Josh, honey, you've been sick out of school for three days and the college is a long drive. We won't be home until very late! Besides, Cammie adores you. It will be just fine."

Joshua knew there was no arguing his way out of this. His parents were taking Anica to her most important piano recital of the year at the state college a little over sixty miles away. The weather was turning bad, so they were getting an early start, before dinnertime. That meant Joshua would have to eat Cammie's cooking, something he didn't look forward to. He looked forward less to having to go to bed at 8:30 per Mom's orders, and having to listen to that junk that his longtime babysitter liked to watch on TV. She would hover around him all evening, look in on him after he went to bed, and generally make his life miserable until his parents got home.

As he sulked in his room, the doorbell rang.

Great.

Cammie.

Cammie lived a few blocks away. She was a senior in high school now, and she had babysat for him and

Anica since he was eight. She was tall and big boned. She had coarse brown hair that she usually kept tied back. She played every varsity sport a girl could play at her school. Anica loved her. Joshua thought she was homely and much too bossy. When Joshua emerged from his room and padded down the stairs, she was taking off her coat. She wore dull red sweats with her school's name on them. As usual, her hair was tied back. Joshua thought it looked like a broom.

He hadn't seen her in a while. Her sweats were tight on her, and her body looked solid. She had not changed much, but he had. Joshua revised his view of her somewhat, thinking she was kind of okay looking, but he still thought she was too bossy.

"There's my Josh!" she exclaimed when he entered the living room. She quickly crossed to give him a hug. Joshua hated her hugs, but this time he kind of liked it. She was warm, and he needed the affection even though he did not think as much. Still, her arms were strong and he could barely breathe.

Outside, snow had begun to fall. The weatherman on TV had said they would probably get around three inches from the storm, but from the way it was coming down, it looked like it would be more.

Anica's recital was at 7:30, and Dad said they had to leave now if they were to make it on time. Joshua's heart sank as he watched his family pile into Dad's Ford Explorer for the trip. He wished they didn't have

to leave so early, but his dad insisted they would need
the time to make it there before the recital. Joshua
counted the hours in his head. The college was sixty-
five miles away, more than an hour's drive on a good
day. The recital and reception wouldn't be over until
after 9:00. With the weather so bad, that meant the
earliest his parents would be home would be close to
midnight. Eight hours. With Cammie.

The time passed slowly, but it wasn't quite as bad as
he'd expected. Cammie let him stay in his room with
his iPad, which was all right since he'd been sick, his
mom had told her, but he could not close the door. The
sound of Cammie's voice on her phone, the stupid
laugh tracks from those stupid comedies she liked,
echoed up the stairwell loud enough to annoy Joshua
even with his earbuds in. At least it was better than
sitting on the sofa with her, watching them.

Cammie came up the stairs to put him to bed at
8:30 on the dot, even though it was Friday and he
usually got to stay up until 10. Cammie turned out his
light and closed his door. Privacy at last! He took out
his iPad from under the bed to watch an R-rated movie
on Netflix, using a password Kevin had given him.

When the movie was over, he got up to go to the
bathroom. Standing at the top of the stairs, he heard
Cammie answering her cell.

"They closed Route 6?" She exclaimed. Joshua
could not hear the voice on the other end of the call,

but he knew it was his mother calling. Joshua could see from the snow on his windowsill that the storm was going to drop a lot more than three inches. This meant his parents would be home even later. It got worse.

"Tomorrow morning? Let me call my mom and I'll call you right back."

Cammie made a quick call to her mother and explained that Joshua's parents and sister were snowed in and staying at a motel for the night. After a few more moments, she called Joshua's mother back.

"Hi, Mrs. Miller, Mom said it was fine for me to stay overnight with Joshua. They canceled practice tomorrow, so I can stay here until you make it home ... Oh, no, the sofa will be fine! Ani's room is just too pretty, and the bed is kinda small ... around noon you think? ... What should I get him for breakfast? ... His math workbook? Okay."

Joshua cringed. This was becoming a nightmare. He went into the bathroom as the conversation ended. He'd wanted to shout to his mother in protest, but it would have been useless.

Unable to sleep, Joshua lay on top of his bed, thinking bitterly about how he wanted to go sledding tomorrow instead of having to stay here with Cammie doing math! Mom would probably keep him in anyway, since he was still getting over his bout with the flu, but he could still hope.

Cammie was on her cell again. He could not make out anything she was saying, but he could hear her voice getting louder, more strident, even frantic. Who was she talking to? There were a few minutes of silence before he heard her again. This time she was sobbing, and that turned into crying incessantly.

Joshua stood up and put his slippers on. He picked up the Kleenex from his night table and left his room, making his way downstairs. Cammie sat on the sofa, a rumpled blanket next to her. She had removed her sweatshirt and her jersey, sitting there in her basketball shorts and her bra. Joshua hesitated on the stairs. Cammie looked up at him through her tears and quickly pulled the blanket up to cover her chest.

"Joshua!" she said curtly. "What are you doing out of bed?"

"I, uh, C-Cammie, I, uh, you were, were crying and I just thought..."

Cammie noticed the box of tissues Joshua carried. She gave into her crying again, but she held her arm out to him, signaling him to join her on the sofa. Joshua sat beside her and offered her the tissues. She took several, blew her nose, and started dabbing at her tears. She had let go of the blanket, and once again, she sat there in her bra. Joshua put his hand lightly on her shoulder. She turned to him and took him tightly into her arms, pulling him close to her chest, kissing the top of his head.

"Oh, Joshua!," she sobbed. "My Josh, my little Josh, you are so, so sweet! You are so, so sweet!"

She held Joshua's face pressed against one of the cups of her bra. It excited him in spite of the sincerity of his efforts to console her. She continued to hold him tightly until her sobbing diminished and stopped. She mopped up the rest of her tears, keeping her arm around him more loosely while he remained close to her. Joshua was clearly aroused and immensely embarrassed.

"I'm sorry, Cammie," he said.

Cammie laughed and tousled his hair. "It's okay, Joshua. Girls know about these things. It happens a lot with boys your age, especially when they're with girls. I guess I should have kept my jersey on. Don't worry about it." She put on her jersey and draped the blanket around her shoulders.

"Cammie, when I came downstairs, why were you crying? What happened?"

Her face became a mask of pain, but she kept control of herself.

"That was my boyfriend on the phone. He was..." She began to sob again. "He's not my boyfriend anymore. He says he just doesn't feel that way about me. And, I, we, were together in bed quite a few times."

Joshua felt something clutching at his heart. Rejection. He knew about that.

"He dumped you over the phone? What a jerk!" Joshua exclaimed angrily. "And he's an idiot! You're so hot!"

Cammie gathered him into her strong arms again and held him tightly.

"Well, you're not a jerk, Joshua Miller. You won't ever be a jerk. Some girl is going to be very lucky to have you for a boyfriend."

Joshua gave her a troubled frown. "Nobody likes me, Cammie. I'm so stupid that girls won't even look at me."

Cammie took his shoulders and looked him in the eye. "The right girl will, Joshua. You'll know her when you meet her."

Joshua seemed comforted, or at least flattered, by her words, but he was still troubled.

"What do I do then?" he said. Cammie tousled his hair again and sighed.

"They haven't told you anything, have they?"

Joshua explained that what little he knew he got from his friend Kevin, who was no older than he. Cammie frowned, and then turned to the picture of Jesus that hung above the sofa. There was one like it in nearly every room of the house. She got up for a moment, took down the picture, and propped it against the wall, Jesus side in.

"Well," she said, "we don't need him for any of this."

109

Cammie started to tell him the facts of life. She explained the workings of his own body and those of her own. Joshua's face reddened.

"Joshua, this is important. I know it's awkward. Boys usually hear about these things from their fathers or they get it in sex ed with a lot of other boys. They opted you out, didn't they?"

"Yeah. My Dad's religion."

"Do you want me to go on? I won't if it's too embarrassing."

"Well, it's kind of uncomfortable, you being a girl and all. But yeah, I want you to go on. I need to know this stuff. It's more embarrassing that I don't."

She affirmed much of what Kevin had told him and what he'd figured out on his own. Joshua was becoming more comfortable. He had known Cammie for a long time, and despite some of the things he'd thought and said about her, he trusted her. She was explaining things she would not talk about with a little boy, and that made him see her in a different light. That made him see her as a friend.

She told him about pregnancy and contraception. She told him about the diseases he could catch and how to prevent them. The biological stuff wasn't too hard for him. The emotional stuff was more important.

"Joshua, you should never have sex with a girl just because she's available or because she comes on to you. You're not that kind of boy. You're going to feel

110

something inside long after it's over. So don't have sex with a girl unless you really like her and you know she likes you."

Joshua understood. He was crazy about girls, but he wanted more from them than just sex.

Cammie looked him in the eye, making sure he had her attention. "And this part is even more important. Whatever you're doing with a girl, no matter how far it's gone, if she says 'no' or 'stop,' she means it. I don't think I have to tell you that, but it's something you have to remember. Always, every time. And Josh? When you meet a girl, never, ever lie to her about anything, unlike a certain person you're helping me to get over. And don't try to hide your feelings. If you like each other, you won't have to."

"I like you, Cammie. Does that mean we should, you know...?" Joshua did not how he wanted her to answer. Cammie smiled.

"Joshua, it's okay to be intimate with the right girl. I'm not the right girl, I'm too old for you, and besides – it's always okay not to. Now, mister, let's get you back to bed. You're still getting over the flu."

Cammie accompanied him back to his room and tucked him in the way she had when he was eight. She kissed him gently on his forehead and left, closing his door behind her.

When morning came, Joshua awoke to the smell of bacon frying in the kitchen. He put on his slippers and made his way downstairs. As he entered the kitchen, Cammie stood at the stove, wearing her same faded red sweats and his mother's slippers.

"Cammie, I, uh..." Joshua wanted to tell her a lot, about how grateful he was, about how wrong he'd been about her.

"Do you want toast or Eggos?" she asked cheerfully.

"Um, Eggos."

She had let him sleep in until almost 10. His family would be home soon. Cammie went about her morning almost like his mother, cleaning up the breakfast dishes, stripping Joshua's bed and putting it in with his laundry, and even fishing his hated math workbook from his backpack. He made no protest. He realized she was looking out for him with this, too. He'd just missed a lot of school.

At ten minutes after noon, he heard the garage door cycle and his father's car pulling in. Mom and Anica stepped through into the kitchen where Joshua sat with Cammie, sincerely trying to comprehend the mysteries of lowest common denominators. His father immediately fired up the snowblower and started clearing the eight inches of snow that had accumulated on the driveway and walks.

The day outside was sunny but extremely cold. Anica's cheeks were rosy when she entered, carrying her overcoat in from the car after the long drive.

Something poignant touched him when he saw her face. Ani. She was so beautiful she made his heart leap. He was so happy she was home with him now.

"How did it go at the recital?" he asked her. Anica proudly pulled a bright, red ribbon from a shopping bag she had brought in with her.

"I got second place!" she said excitedly. "I made a couple of mistakes on the Beethoven, but the judges didn't mark too much off."

There was a bright bouquet of flowers in the bag with the ribbon. They had not traveled well, but she hopefully placed them in a vase filled with water, arranging them carefully. Then she was off, happily skipping toward her room, to find a good place for her bright, red ribbon among the other ribbons, medals, and trophies she kept on the crowded shelf above her bed.

He hadn't noticed that Cammie had left the table and was already standing by the front door in her jacket and boots, talking to his mom. Some money changed hands and she and his mom briefly embraced. Joshua ran to the door.

Cammie smiled at him, gave him a big hug, and then said ruefully,

"Best get back to those fractions, little man!" With that, she turned and receded into the arctic cold outside.

113

Josh and Ani

Finished with her homework, Anica went downstairs to begin her piano practice. She retrieved the piece she was rehearsing from the piano bench and spread it out on the music rack. She started with scales to warm up. Joshua came down the stairs a few minutes later.

"Hi, Ani."

"Hi, Josh. Did you come down for a snack? I think dinner will be ready soon."

"No. I came down for you. I want to listen to the second best pianist in the state."

Anica stopped and turned to him. "Seriously?" She asked skeptically.

"Never more serious. Or what serious is for me, anyway. Go on."

Anica laughed. "That was just the F sharp major scale, Josh. I still have ten more to go."

"But I'll bet nobody plays them better."

Anica laughed again. She knew Joshua was joking, but he wasn't being sarcastic. She continued with her warmup exercises until they were finished. She adjusted her seat a little, then started to play the piece her teacher had given her to practice. She fumbled a phrase after eight bars and cursed to herself mildly. She backed up to the beginning of the piece and started over. This time, she played the right notes and

114

got almost halfway through the fifth page before she had to stop and back up a few bars again.

"What's that you're playing?" Joshua asked. Anica had almost forgotten he was there.

"It's the First Piano Sonata by Robert Schumann. Mrs. Ilyanovich wants me to learn it for my spring recital."

"I like it, but it sounds kind of sad."

Anica realized Joshua was serious. It was in keeping with the way he had been acting recently. She did not know what had come over him, but it was nice.

"Go on, Ani. I'd like to hear the rest of it."

"It's kind of long. I'm just working on the first movement now."

"You'll have to tell me about that stuff. Like, I don't think I know what a sonata is."

"It's a long piece for a single instrument, or sometimes a few instruments. They have movements, like symphonies. It gets kind of complicated."

"That's okay, Ani. I just want to hear you play some more."

Joshua was endearing himself to his sister by the minute. She went back to playing, making fewer mistakes as she learned the style and mood of the piece. When she got to the end of the first movement, she stopped.

"That's all I'm going to do today," she told Joshua. "It's a difficult piece. I think Mrs. Ilyanovich wants to challenge me."

"I think she knows you can do it. I know you can. That was really nice. I want to hear it again, maybe the rest of it next time."

"You're being too nice to me," Anica said modestly.

"No, I mean it, Ani. And now I know what a sonata is." Joshua continued, "Say, don't you have a meet this Saturday? I don't think I've seen you do your gymnastics since you were six. Can I come? I don't know anything about that stuff, either."

Anica put her music back into the piano bench as their mother called them in for dinner. Joshua rose from his chair to follow her. Anica turned around to face him. She crossed to him and put her arms around him. Joshua returned her embrace and held her tightly. Neither of them wanted to let go.

"Hey, you two, your dinner is getting…" Agnes entered the living room to behold her children. She retreated quietly into her kitchen, moved to tears.

Becky

Becky Lindstrom frowned at the outfits arrayed side by side on her bed. What could she wear today? Not the fuzzy green sweater and black leggings, she had worn that last week. The denim skirt? That meant leggings again, and she decided she would rather wear jeans today, but which ones? She chewed on her lower lip a little. She had many pairs of jeans but there were only a few that she liked. She had worn them all within the last two weeks and she wanted something different.

"Damn this awful winter!" she cursed in dismay. It was so much easier to dress in the warmer months. She had many pairs of very flattering, very short shorts that she liked to wear. She had lots of cute tops and T-shirts, and short skirts with shorts or linings built into them.

She could wear none of them today. The forecast was for a high of 10°. Even though she got a ride to and from school, it was cold outside in the pickup lane and it was too uncomfortable even to wear the distressed jeans she liked. They had threadbare spots in strategic places, but they let in the wind.

Becky had light blond hair that hung below her shoulders, and periwinkle blue eyes. Boys had been falling all over themselves around her for as long as she could remember. She enjoyed the way it made her

117

feel, but it wasn't without problems. The nice boys were so sheepish around her. The ones her friends liked were privileged or athletic, and they often looked down on the less popular kids. She hated that. She knew she was pretty, even that she was very pretty, but she wasn't vain.

She often thought her mother was. She couldn't understand what was so important about designer clothes, boutique hair salons, professional manicures, and spending half an hour on makeup in the morning. Her mother would spend hours at an expensive health club, working out on machines, but she scarcely did anything active and fun outdoors. Exercise for her was just another thing she had to do to be attractive.

Her mother was beautiful, but she acted as though it was something that had to cost money. As soon as Becky entered puberty, her mother began trying to convince her of the same. Of late, she had wanted Becky to try a little lip gloss, but she didn't think it looked right on her and it left a mark on her glass when she got something to drink. She painted her nails for fun, but she kept them short. Becky just wanted to be a girl. She would grow up soon enough. All she had inherited of her mother's disposition was having a hard time deciding what to wear.

She had been moving about her room clad in pastel blue panties and a matching, lightly padded bra, with lace around the edges. There was not a boy on earth who wouldn't give something dear to see her that way, but all she wanted now was something cute to put on over it. The clock read 7:30. She had been trying to decide on an outfit for the last half hour, but could take no more time. She settled on a pair of faded jeans with patches on the knees and a blue chiffon sweater she hadn't worn in a while. Not the look she wanted, but it would have to do if she was to make it to school on time.

The Lindstroms lived in the most well-to-do corner of the area served by Truman Junior High. They had a large, five-bedroom brick house, on a shady cul-de-sac. Her father was a prominent lawyer. Her mother mostly went out during the day to spend his money, of which there was no shortage. The house was lavishly furnished, but to Becky, it was just home, a home that was empty too much of the time. Her mother would drive her to school in her flashy Mercedes SL, but it was just a car. She never thought very much about the things she had, but she did not, like her mother, bemoan the things she didn't have. She wanted for nothing, but asked for little from her parents. The only things she really wanted were some siblings and a cat.

Material things. It seemed like her mother lived for them. New clothes. New furnishings. New hairdos. She was always shopping for something or another, or going to get her nails done, or going to a place where they gave her a white bathrobe and put green mud on

119

her face. Sometimes she tried to get Becky to come with her when she picked her up from school, but Becky would tell her she was thinking of going over to Natalie's house, or Erin's house, or Caitlin's house, or that she had too much homework.

She took tennis lessons twice a week, and she was a good player. Her mother was always trying to get her to switch to cheer, or dance, or something else "more feminine," as she put it, but she had started playing tennis with her father when she was six, and she loved it. It gave her pretty legs and put a spring in her step. She loved being outdoors in the sunlight, unlike her mother. When it was cold or rainy, she worked with her coach on the indoor courts at the club where her father played golf. Her dad still played spirited matches with her on the courts there, and she enjoyed the time it gave them together. How could she have that, prancing about in a tutu or jumping up and down with pom poms? She thought it was silly.

Most other days she spent afternoons at home by herself. She would chat or text with Natalie or Erin or Caitlin, or any of her other friends, but it seemed to her that they were all becoming more like her mother with each passing year. She wished that she had more friends, friends who were not like Natalie and Erin and Caitlin, who were popular but often catty and proud.

Becky was very much her own girl, a free spirit who didn't feel a need to conform. But life in middle school sometimes felt like a trap. Who else could she run with but other pretty girls that everyone seemed to like, or wanted to be like. It had been that way since she'd moved here from California with her parents when she was eight.

On her debut at Lincolncrest Elementary School, the boys instantly started falling all over themselves around her, and the other pretty, popular girls flocked to seek her friendship. Becky was outgoing and infectiously cheerful, with an impish sense of humor. She was very bright and a good student. It did not take long before everyone knew who she was, but the friends she had then were the friends she had now. The new friends she had made this year were a lot like them.

She was nice to everybody, including the kids her popular friends did not approve of, but everyone seemed to follow some unwritten code, who's in and who's out. The out kids seemed to lead more interesting lives, but it wasn't easy for her to get to know them. They probably assumed she was shallow and stuck up, she thought, even though she tried hard not to act like it. She would just have to try harder, she told herself.

Most of the Lincolncrest kids had come here to Truman. She knew many of them and always said hello. There was this one boy, though. Jeffrey? Jeremy? Her first year at Lincolncrest, she had been in

121

Mrs. Marcus's class with him, but she didn't quite recall his name. She remembered that his attention wandered a lot. He got picked on by the teacher, and many of the other kids, because he didn't pay attention in class and could never finish his work on time. He was cute, but he never smiled, and he was so quiet.

Like the other boys, he often looked at her, but he never spoke to her or any other girl in school. He kept to himself, although he had a cute little sister that he sometimes walked home with. He had only one friend that she could remember, but she didn't think he went to this school now. She had felt badly for him, and didn't like the way he was treated. When she asked her friends about him, they said he had always been quiet and shy, and hardly anyone paid attention to him except the mean kids who liked to pick on him.

Every day, he sat alone in the opposite corner of the cafeteria, often gazing at her. He quickly averted his eyes whenever she raised her head to look back, just as he had at Lincolncrest. She was used to the attention boys gave her, but the way he looked at her – it wasn't creepy at all, she thought, but it was not quite like the looks she usually got. He was obviously attracted to her, but there was something more, something that both flattered her and made her a little sad. She supposed it was because he still seemed so sad, and lonely. Sometimes she thought she should say hello, but whenever he saw her walking his way, he would

122

quickly dart around a corner or cross to the opposite side of the corridor, keeping his eyes on the floor.

His name. Jonah. That had to be it. Wait, no, it was something else, something like it. There was no one she could ask; none of her friends knew him any better than she did. It would come to her, she thought.

When the bell rang for 5th period, she left the cafeteria. Suddenly with a million things to do, she forgot about the sad-eyed boy from Mrs. Marcus's class.

Life was not perfect, but it was good. She just wished she'd had something better to wear today.

123

Joshua

"Hey, Mom!" Kevin called, "Do we have anything by Shoe Man?"

Joey-Lynn Maas stuck her head into Kevin's room. Her short hair was pink at the tips and she had tattoos on her arms and shoulders. Joshua liked her a lot. She never talked down to him like other grownups did, even treated him as a friend. She was pretty and a lot of fun. The only thing he didn't like about her was her cooking. It was all rice and vegetables and sprouts and things that looked like potatoes but didn't taste like them. Kevin said they were vegans, but he was always happy to eat hamburgers and pizza when he visited Joshua's house.

"I don't think so, Kev. Is he a rapper?" she said.

"I don't know, Mom. Josh likes him. What about Spotify?"

Joshua interjected, "No, Kevin! Sorry Mrs. Maas! Schumann. Robert Schumann. One of those classical guys. He's like, you know, two hundred years old or something."

Joey-Lynn took out her iPhone and started pecking at the screen trying to find something for Joshua to listen to. She doted on him like that, which was another reason Joshua liked her. Kevin's father was weird as hell but not the least bit scary like his own father was. He would talk enthusiastically at the dinner

124

table, although Joshua often had no idea what he was talking about. He had a kiln in the basement and their house was full of crazy-looking things he'd made down there.

Kevin's sister Autumn was a sophomore at the college where their father taught. Her ears were pierced so many times Joshua wondered how they didn't fall apart. Like her mother's, her hair was cut short and dyed in crazy colors. She liked Joshua, too, even flirted with him, which made him uncomfortable. She was pretty in spite of what she did to herself. She had a boyfriend, so why did she keep telling him how cute he was? She was way too old for him, older than Cammie, even.

She called out from her room down the hall. "I think Dad has some Stravinsky on vinyl. Want me to find it? Hey Josh, do you like Zappa? Dad says he's the greatest composer like, ever!"

Kevin was chagrined. His family treated his best friend better than they treated him, which was not badly at all. "Never mind, Mom! Never mind, Sis! Jeez, Josh, you really listen to that stuff?"

"Ani got me into it. I like it. Schumann, anyway. And Chopin. I like him, too."

"Show Pan? Never heard of him, either. I thought you hated Ani's music."

"Nah. I was just jealous. I like listening to her play. I always did. And we talk all the time now. It's great.

It's back like we were when we were little."

Kevin was pleased. He'd have hugged Joshua if they did that. "Aw, that's way cool, man. Way cool! You finally figure out how cute she is? Hey, d'ya think you can take me to one of her meets?"

"That's probably more than you can handle, Kevin, but I'll ask Mom anyway. She is beautiful, like you keep telling me, but it isn't that. Not just that, anyway. I guess I figured out it was my all my fault. It's not her fault she's smarter than me."

"She's a hell of a lot prettier. Hey, speaking of pretty, how's Becky lookin' this year? You still got a thing for her?"

Joshua rolled his eyes. "What do you think? Remember how she grew her hair out last year? And the way she filled out? It's driving me crazy."

"Wish I'd gone to Truman. Wilson sucks."

"Prolly not as bad as Truman. But yeah, Becky's there. Could be worse."

"You ever gonna talk to her?"

"Way out of my league, Kevin. Kind of like Ani and you."

"Not funny, Josh."

Mary Elizabeth

On a blustery, early April day, Joshua came home from school to find his mother curled up in a corner of the sofa, still in her coat, crying. The coffee table was littered with Kleenexes. She ought to have been at work at this hour. Joshua dropped his backpack and hurried to sit next to her on the sofa.

"Mom? Mom? W-what's wrong? What has happened?"

His mother choked back tears and put her arms around him.

"Grandma Aggie is dead." She could get no more out before she began bawling again. Joshua felt bad for his mom, but he was relieved that it wasn't worse.

Grandma Aggie, as everyone called her, was Mom's grandmother. At last count, and he could not remember when he stopped counting, she was ninety-four years old and had been living in a nursing home since before Joshua was born. He had only seen her once, at a family reunion five years ago. Grandma and Aunt Alice had brought her in a wheelchair to the big yard party where the family had gathered. Mom took him and Anica over to meet her, but she was so addled with dementia she didn't know they were there. Joshua had never seen anyone so old. She scared him. Not long after, she had to go back to the nursing home, and he never saw her again. Mom had not seen her since then, either, as the Miller family did not travel much.

"Josh," his mother sobbed, "We'll have to drive down to Cliffordsborough. The wake is Friday night and the funeral is on Sunday."

Wake? *Wake?* Joshua was petrified at the thought. When his Aunt Adele died three years ago, he had to go to the wake. Joshua didn't even know what a wake was, but when they got to the funeral home and he saw Aunt Adele in her casket, he threw up. His father was furious with him. Never in his short life had Joshua seen anything more dreadful, and now he was going to be dragged to another one. He felt queasy just at the thought. At least he would get out of school on Friday.

When Friday came, mom let him and Anica sleep in a little so they would be rested for the trip. At 10:00 they would pick up Grandma and Aunt Alice. The drive to Cliffordsborough would be a bit over five hours. Dad's 3-row Ford Explorer was the only car big enough to transport everyone. Dad was out of town at an agents' convention and was not coming with them. Joshua wasn't unhappy about that.

Neither was he unhappy about sharing the third row seats with Anica. Mom and Grandma were in the front and Aunt Alice, all 330 pounds of her, took up most of the second row. Not too long ago, having to sit next to his sister for five hours would have been hell. But now...

"Mom! Josh is cheating!" Anica chuckled.

128

"Am not!" Joshua replied, laughing out loud.

"Are too!"

"It's a video game, Mom. You can't cheat!"

Agnes looked back at her children in the rearview mirror. Joshua had brought his iPad and they were playing some kind of game on it. It did her heart good to see them getting along so well. They had been on the road for nearly two hours, and she hadn't heard a single complaint from either of them. The trip seemed to be bringing them even closer together, so perhaps Grandma Aggie was smiling on them from Heaven, happy to have done some good as she left this world.

Agnes stifled a sob. She'd been named after Grandma Aggie, and was very fond of her when she was a child. Everyone was. Agnes came from a big Catholic family. Grandma Aggie had raised six children. Each of her children also had big families when they married, and most of those children – Agnes's cousins – also had lots of kids. Agnes herself was one of five children. She had planned to have more children, and it often saddened her that she could no longer conceive.

Nearly all of the clan would be there – Agnes, Alice, and their brothers, their wives, her nieces and nephews, her aunts and uncles, their children and grandchildren - Agnes had twenty-nine cousins and was not sure how many children they'd had. The family reunion a few years back was so large she hadn't been able to count them all.

Cliffordsborough was a large town near the state's southern border. Grandma had been born and raised there, and a lot of Agnes's relatives still lived there. When they arrived, they went straight to the funeral home where Grandma Aggie lay in state. Joshua donned his uncomfortable suit coat and clip-on tie when they stepped out of the car. Anica, who looked so pretty in her black velvet dress, straightened his lapels and tried to tug the sleeves of his jacket down over his cuffs.

The funeral home resembled an imposing Gothic mansion. There was a huge porch that wrapped around the front and one side of the building. The early spring weather was mild and pleasant, and many people were gathered there, chatting, drinking coffee, occasionally embracing. He knew his uncles and their children. Others were vaguely familiar to him, but the rest he didn't know even though he was related to most of them. Grandma Aggie's wake was so large, the family had reserved the entire building. Two large rooms on the second floor were reserved for food and drink, and the few other rooms were empty.

They spent a few moments on the porch as the adults greeted some of the family members. Joshua braced himself as they entered the foreboding mansion, glad that he'd eaten nothing on the trip. Grandma had been escorted inside to take her place at

130

the head of the receiving line. She was to join her five siblings and Aggie's only surviving brother, a man in his 80s who got around with a walker. The line was so long it extended into the entrance hall, then into a large side room that would open up onto the big room where Aggie was propped up in her coffin. When Joshua was finally able to see her, much of his anxiety melted away. She didn't look much different dead than she had alive, if she had indeed been alive when he first saw her. A pair of glasses with very thick lenses had been placed on her face. Joshua found this puzzling and morbidly comical. What would she need them for?

A lot of the people were kneeling and crossing themselves when they got to the casket. Mom did the same, even though she hadn't been a practicing Catholic since her father died. Joshua and Anica did not kneel, but they tried to look respectful when passing, stopping just long enough to take a cursory view of Aggie's bony corpse. This was disconcerting, but he felt a little better when Anica's hand slipped into his.

They paused to hug their grandmother and greet the other old people who stood on the other side of the coffin from the receiving line. The little man with the walker shook Joshua's hand with a surprisingly strong grip. Anica took both of his hands and gave him a small kiss on the cheek, which he appreciated very much. When they had passed the next of kin, a frail woman with red hair led them both upstairs. Joshua recognized her, no doubt from the last time he visited Cliffordsborough.

There were two big rooms at the top of the stairs. In one of them, a crowd of adults stood talking and drinking. There was a good deal of laughter. There was an open bar at the end of the room, with a red-vested bartender busily serving up drinks. The minister at his father's church had said drinking was a sin, but evidently these Catholics had a different idea. Joshua started wishing he were Catholic, even though he'd vowed to never set foot inside a church again when he was old enough to move out of the house.

The other room was nearly bursting at the seams with children ranging in age from preschoolers to teens. There was a table filled with salads, sandwiches, wraps, french fries, sliced ham, fried chicken, mashed potatoes, soups, and cooked vegetables. Another table held a variety of cakes, pies, brownies, torts, cookies, and a large punch bowl filled with something red that had pineapple rings and maraschino cherries floating on top. Joshua realized he was very hungry and headed straight for the food table. Anica quickly struck up a conversation with one of Uncle Alan's daughters and disappeared into the crowd with her.

Joshua took a plate and surveyed the table. He took a sandwich and some fries, and was looking at the rest of the hot dishes when a girl sidled up next to him.

"The ham is dry but the chicken is alright. Try the oatmeal cookies, too."

Joshua looked around to see if she could be talking to someone else. He wasn't used to girls talking to him.

"Joshua? It's me, Mary Elizabeth. Mary Elizabeth Connor. We met at the reunion. Do you remember me?" She laid a hand lightly on his forearm. Joshua was even less used to girls touching him, but he didn't mind at all.

Mary Elizabeth Connor was a little older than he and a grade ahead of him in school. When he saw her face, he remembered her right away, and then he remembered where he had seen the red-haired woman who escorted his sister and him up the stairs, at the family reunion.

He remembered the day clearly. Mom, Anica, and him had just arrived at a big house that belonged to his great uncle. Anica was invited to join a group of little girls in a parlor just inside the door, while Joshua and his mother made their way to the back yard, where most of the people were. Mom spied one of her cousins nearby.

"Irene!" his mother called. A red-haired woman smiled as Mom led him over to a shade tree where she stood. A cute, chubby little girl stood by bashfully, half-hiding behind her mother. She had short red hair like her mother's, and sea-green eyes that he thought were very pretty. She easily drew a smile from Joshua, and she smiled back, moving a little more behind her mother as she did so.

The two women introduced them and ordered them to go find something to do together. Joshua liked her immediately. She was even shyer than he was, but it was nice to have someone to play with. There were mobs of children around, but they had already clustered into groups when he arrived and it was hard for Joshua to approach them.

She didn't talk to him at first, but she kept glancing bashfully at him, and when he smiled at her, she smiled back. He loved her smile. She had freckles and dimples in her face, and her green eyes sparkled. He didn't see her chubbiness, it was easy to look past it. They went to the food table together, and she sat down on the grass with him after they filled their plates. She looked unhappy after they were seated, cross-legged on the lawn. Joshua asked her,

"Mary? What's wrong?"

"Mary *Elizabeth*," she corrected him. "I forgot my lemonade." Joshua promptly went back to the food table to get her some. When he returned, she smiled up at him. She kept smiling at him as they ate their potato salad and cookies, but she seemed a little uncomfortable when they finished eating. Joshua decided his mission for the rest of the day was to make this girl smile. He took both of their plates and their cups and walked them over to a nearby trash basket.

When he returned, he held out his hand to her.

"Hey, that looks like fun!" he said, pointing to a bounce house set up in the corner of the yard.

"Come on, Mary *Elizabeth*, let's go check it out!" She took his hand and he helped her up. She smiled at him again, and he just kept it going the rest of the day. The more he could make her smile, the more fun he had, and he was really, really sorry when he had to leave. She stood in front of his great uncle's house with her mother, waving to him as his mom was driving away. Joshua thought he saw tears in her eyes and he was holding back tears of his own. He could not remember when he'd had a nicer day.

Now she looked a lot different. Good different. Her wavy red hair hung past her shoulders, and she had those same sparkling green eyes. There was a sprinkling of freckles across her nose. Her ears were pierced, and she wore in them a pair of pretty tourmaline earrings. She was still slightly chubby, but not in a way that Joshua found at all displeasing. She wore a dark green skirt and a matching, unbuttoned cardigan over a lighter green satin blouse that fit her snugly. Her breasts were not large, but the tightness of her blouse made them stand out. Her legs were bare below her skirt, which ended just above her knees. She wore black ballet flats that were scuffed at the toes. Joshua had never before met anyone so beautiful.

She was standing closer to him than any girl other

135

than his sister ever had. She was in no hurry to remove her hand from his arm, and he didn't want her to. Her presence took on a kind of glow, while everything and everyone else in the crowded room seemed to recede into the shadows. He looked into her lovely green eyes and she was looking back into his. He had never been able to look into a girl's eyes for more than a split second before averting his gaze, but he found that now he couldn't look away.

"I'm going to get some cookies," She told him. "It's too stuffy and crowded in here. Come on, there's a bench outside that nobody's using."

Joshua quickly took a handful of cookies and a paper cup filled with the red punch, while Mary Elizabeth filled a small plate with cookies, one of each variety on the dessert table. She led him down a staircase different from the one he'd come up. It led past an empty corridor to a foyer with an ornate glass door that opened onto a small, deserted garden bordered with tall hedges. There was a statue of the Virgin Mary in the center, encircled with marble benches. Joshua took a seat on one of them, and Mary Elizabeth sat down next to him. Joshua felt something strange and new and wonderful. He'd never been alone with a girl before, and she seemed to get prettier every time he looked at her.

He was still very hungry. He had picked at his breakfast, and his stomach was queasy when Mom stopped at the highway oasis on the way here. He took a couple of bites from his sandwich, but it had cucumbers, which he hated, so he just ate his fries. He'd taken six oatmeal cookies from the table, and Mary Elizabeth had been right, they were very good. He finished them quickly.

Mary Elizabeth sat with her plate of cookies in her lap, eating each one slowly. Seeing that Joshua had finished his, she offered,

"Here, take some of mine. I don't think I can finish them all." Joshua bumped her elbow as she was handing him the plate, and they almost spilled onto the bench. She laughed a little, then moved away from him. As she did so, she threw a leg over to straddle the bench so she could face him. Joshua straddled the bench himself so he could better see her face. He very much enjoyed seeing her face.

Mary Elizabeth set the plate of cookies between them and they ate them until they were gone. He raised his head to look at her face again. Her eyes once again met his and held them. The mesmerizing glow he'd seen before returned, brighter this time, radiant, almost blinding. He could not raise his guard. She was looking into his very soul, seeing things in him of which he was not even aware, and all of it was hers for the taking. It overwhelmed him, and after a few seconds, he blinked and lowered his head. She could sense his nervousness and she frowned a little.

"Are you still hungry?" she said. "Do you want to go back inside?"

"No, it's really nice out here. With you." Joshua realized this was the first time he had spoken to her since she introduced herself. He had answered her earnestly, without stammering, not caring to conceal how he felt. She had seen so much in his eyes that she already knew.

Mary Elizabeth smiled again. She took Joshua's plate and set it atop the empty plate between them, then set both plates behind her. She moved closer to him, close enough that her knees touched his. It was a little disconcerting at first, and he felt a little better when Mary Elizabeth modestly put her hands on her skirt.

"Did you know Grandma Aggie?" she asked.

"No," said Joshua. "Mom took me and Ani over to meet her when we came to the reunion, but she didn't know we were there. I was kind of scared. What about you?"

"Yeah," she said, "I live here. Mom used to visit her about twice a month and she'd take me along once in a while. Aggie wasn't like that all the time. Sometimes she would smile at me and say something nice, but she always called me by my mother's name."

"Your mom was?"

"Grandma Aggie was her grandmother."

"Yeah, she was my mom's grandmother, too."

Joshua was downhearted. So he and Mary Elizabeth were related. But of course they were, why else would he have seen her here and at the reunion?

"So you and me, we're cousins?"

"Second cousins," she said. She added, brightly, "Did you know second cousins can even get married?"

She knew his every thought, and she knew just what to say. His mood brightened and he found himself relaxing. She was so easy to talk to. Joshua could not remember the last time he really talked to any girl other than Anica. Then he did remember. It was this same girl, all those years ago. Now they were here in this garden together, with no one else around, the sun setting over the hedges, and she was so bright and fresh and pretty.

They talked and laughed until it was nearly dark. Some lights recessed into the ground came on, illuminating the statue and the undersides of the benches. As darkness fell, the temperature dropped. Mary Elizabeth shifted her legs back over the side of the bench and buttoned her cardigan. Joshua did the same, buttoning his jacket. She stood up.

"It's getting chilly," she said. "Maybe we should go back inside."

It was indeed getting cold, but Joshua didn't want to leave this magical place. Mary Elizabeth took his hand and he stood up from the bench. Then she took his other hand and moved in close to him. Without a shred of nervousness, he leaned forward and kissed her. She leaned into him and kissed him back. And then her arms were around his neck, and his were around her waist. The mystical glow around her engulfed him and he began to glow with it. He felt warm and comfortable despite the chill in the air. She made him feel so at ease. He forgot he was shy. He forgot he was a loser. She made him feel worthy, accepted, even...

Even loved.

"Let's go inside," she said. "I know a place where we can go."

Holding his hand, she led him back inside the funeral home, down a long hall that led to another staircase, and up to the second floor. The landing opened up into a hallway with two sets of double doors with signs that said "Caterer's Entrance"

Mary Elizabeth opened one of them, and they entered a banquet room similar to the one he'd been in earlier. It was empty, softly illuminated by wall sconces. Around the room were a number of upholstered chairs and some large sofas.

"The other door is locked. No one will come in here," she told him.

Mary Elizabeth stepped out of her shoes and removed her cardigan, dropping it on a chair near the door they came in. Joshua discarded his ill-fitting jacket and tossed it on the same chair. Mary Elizabeth undid the top button of her blouse, and then she playfully removed Joshua's clip-on tie and undid the top button of Joshua shirt, relieving him of the discomfort of its stiff collar.

She had revealed only as much as modesty allowed, but the more Joshua saw of her, the more he liked what he saw. Joshua observed that she had a sprinkling of freckles on her chest as well as her nose. He wanted to count them all, as he loved every one of them. Around her neck, she wore a silver chain with a small Catholic crucifix.

She took him by the hand to one of the sofas. She sat down on the edge, still holding his hand, and he sat down close to her. She put her arms around his neck.

"Now ... ," she said, "where were we?"

She smiled and looked deeply into his eyes. He gazed into hers, once again losing himself in them, losing himself in her. He trusted her completely, abandoning his guard and glad to be rid of it. There was nothing he cared to keep from her. He was hers to do with as she wished.

Mary Elizabeth had found him. She had led him into the garden, and she had led him here. She wanted to be with him. This beautiful girl wanted to be alone with him. Right now, he wanted nothing more than to be with her. Joshua didn't know being with a girl, this girl, could be like this. Attraction and desire were not new to him, but there was something far more powerful present.

He loved her. He was sure of it at the moment her eyes first met his. She held him closely, and the glow engulfed them again, bright and warm and comfortable. She had come into his life to set it right. He wanted to dissolve himself in her, leaving behind his doubts and fears, the years of believing he was inferior, defective, worthless. He wanted to belong to her, to die in her arms so that she could give him life anew.

They kissed again, alone together in the softly lit room. There was excitement, but no nervousness. There was passion, but no urgency. Most of all, there was love. Joshua was as certain of her love as he was of his own. Neither of them had to say anything. No words could express what both of them could feel.

Together on the sofa, they lost track of time. They went only as far as they wanted to go, knowing that this was new to both of them. All that mattered was that they had each other. Joshua realized that he had found someone – someone loved him.

In that moment, the years of loneliness, years of rejection, years of doubt, years of pain, all melted away. In that moment, Joshua's life changed forever, and he had never been more at peace with the world or more content with himself. The magic of this one night made up for every way in which the world had ever mistreated him.

After an hour – or was it two – Joshua found

something to say. "I love you, Mary Elizabeth."
Joshua told her. "I'm sure of it."

Mary Elizabeth held him more tightly.

"I love you, too, Joshua. I knew it right away."

They held each other for a while longer, neither of
them saying anything, until Mary Elizabeth asked,

"Joshua? Have you been in love before?"

Joshua half-smiled. "Oh, there's this girl at my
school. I've known her since the third grade. Well, that
isn't right, I know who she is, and I can't help looking
at her. She's pretty. She doesn't really know me, so
no, I've never been in love before. I know what that is
now, and I'm glad. I'm glad it's you. I knew it right
away, too, when I first looked into your eyes. What
about you?"

"There was a boy last summer. He was older, in
high school, on the football team with my brother. I
was so naive. He took advantage of me. It lasted a
little over a month. My father was furious when he
found out I was seeing him. He told him, and his
parents, that he had better never come near me again.
He didn't know how far it had gone, or he would have
done worse."

"That must have hurt." Joshua said softly.

"At first, yes. But then I found out he had a
reputation, and that I wasn't the only seventh grader
he'd conquered. It was something he bragged about to
his friends. After that, I didn't want to see him or even

143

hear his name again."

Mary Elizabeth kissed him and looked into his eyes. "I was afraid he'd damaged me, that he'd taken something from me that I could never get back. But here you are, Joshua, and everything is so right now. So right."

They continued to hold one another closely, silent for many more minutes, before Mary Elizabeth spoke again,

"It's almost 9:00. We should go back with the others."

Joshua did not want to leave, but he knew she was right. His mother was probably looking for him. They put themselves back together and left their secret place.

Mary Elizabeth led him back down the stairs, but took yet another route, one that led to a side door that opened onto a deserted area of the wraparound porch. Before, it had not occurred to him to ask her,

"Hey, how come you know this place so well?"

She gestured to a small sign beside the side door they'd used. It read:

Angus Connor and Sons
Funeral Directors

"My dad and his brothers own it. I kind of grew up here. Dad never lets me go into the basement – that's where they fix them up – but I pretty much know every inch of the rest of this place."

"That seems kind of spooky. Doesn't it bother you, you know, dead people?"

"Not when you grow up around it, but I totally get it. Everybody dies, but no one wants to be reminded of it." she told him. "It's really pretty hard. I don't have a lot of friends. Other kids think I'm weird."

Joshua didn't understand how such a pretty girl could be unpopular, but he could relate.

"Yeah, other kids avoid me too. My dad just sells insurance and my mom works for some people who build houses. But me, I guess I am kind of weird."

Mary Elizabeth took both of his hands and kissed him.

"I think you're kind of sweet," she told him, then kissed him again. She continued,

"I wondered. You were all by yourself in a crowded room and you seemed lonely. I thought you could use a friend, so I came over."

"So that's what we are?" said Joshua, "Friends?"

She kissed him again, long enough to give him his answer. There was no tension between them at all. He had known her for just a few hours, but it seemed to him that he'd known her since the beginning of time.

They made their way around to the front of the building where a few people were gathered on the porch despite the chilly night air. Among them was

145

Anica, her arms crossed against the chill.

"Josh! Josh! Where have you been? Mom and Aunt Alice are looking all over for you!" Her eyebrows furrowed, and she added, "Who's your friend?"

This was awkward. Joshua fumbled with his words.

"Um, ah, Ani, Ani, this is Mary Elizabeth. She's my, our cousin.

"Second cousin," Mary Elizabeth interjected.

"She lives here in Cliffordsborough. She was just showing me around. Mary Elizabeth, this is my sister Anica."

Anica looked peeved. *Is she jealous?!* Joshua thought.

Mary Elizabeth held out her hand. When Anica reluctantly took it, she moved in to lightly embrace her.

"So you're Ani! Joshua told me so much about you. He says you play the piano so beautifully, and you're a really good gymnast, too, and so smart. He told me you were very pretty, but I didn't realize how much until just now."

Anica's expression softened into a blushing smile. Mary Elizabeth had a way of winning people over, Joshua thought. He was more bewildered than ever, angry even, that she didn't have more friends. Why would it matter what her father did for a living?

They entered the funeral home together, where he found Mom, Aunt Alice, and the woman with red hair

146

waiting in the foyer. Joshua thought his mother would be angry with him, but she said instead,

"Josh, there you are! Mary Elizabeth, dear, do you remember me? I'm Agnes, Agnes Miller, your mother's cousin. I'm Joshua's mother. Your mom told me she'd seen you together earlier. It's so nice that you and Joshua could get acquainted again."

Mary Elizabeth turned to the red-haired woman and said,

"Hi Mom. I was just showing Joshua around."

"That was really nice of you, dear, but we have to get going. Most of the people have already left and your father wants to start taking things down."

Mary Elizabeth turned to leave with her mother, but she suddenly stopped, turned, and gave Joshua a warm, lengthy hug.

"Goodnight, Joshua. I'll see you on Sunday."

Joshua watched as they left, disappearing around a corner. A few minutes later, a silver gray sedan pulled out of the parking lot. Before it turned to enter the busy street in front of the funeral home, a rear window rolled down. Mary Elizabeth stuck her head out and waved at him. Joshua raised his hand to wave back, but the car pulled out into the street and was gone.

Sunday, Joshua thought. Why not tomorrow? All Joshua could think about in the car on the way to the motel was how he ached to see her again. It must have shown on his face. Anica turned to him and gently

147

touched his cheek. Joshua turned his head to look into her big brown eyes.

"You really like her, don't you?" Anica said, a trace of jealousy in her voice. Joshua smiled.

"Yeah. Yeah, I do. Ani, I've never met a girl like her before. I never thought there was a girl like her before."

A tear came to his eye as he recalled the image of her waving to him from her mother's car. Anica took a Kleenex from her handbag and gently wiped it away. She did not speak again, but she reached over to hold his hand and held it the rest of the way to the motel. Her touch soothed him and tugged at his heart.

Ani. He loved her so much, yet he'd just fallen in love, deeply in love, with Mary Elizabeth.

When Saturday morning came, Mom told him and Anica they were going to meet up with Uncle Alan and his brood to visit a nearby tourist attraction, a large caverns where you could ride in a boat underground. Joshua asked about Mary Elizabeth.

"Irene told me they were all going to a big hospital in St. Louis. Irene sees a specialist there and he wants to run some tests on her and her children. They'll be gone all day, I'm afraid."

Why didn't she tell me? Is she sick? Her whole family? Joshua worried. Dejection clawed at him, but Ani was here, and the thought of sitting together on a slow boat ride through the caverns sounded nice.

148

The caverns were located in the rolling hills south of Cliffordsborough. They met up with Uncle Alan and Aunt Claire and their five children to take the boat tour. Joshua and Anica sat together in the aftmost seat as the boat began its voyage through the beautiful and strange rock formations underground. Although the weather above was mild, the air in the caverns was damp and chilly. Joshua and Anica had worn their hoodies, but they still sat close together, Joshua keeping an arm around his sister to keep her warm. Her warmth, in turn, comforted Joshua against the chill.

Anica felt a sense of wonder at the sights. Stalactites hung above them, sometimes descending almost close enough to touch. She excitedly pointed out some of the interesting features they encountered, and Joshua acknowledged her remarks with approval. His mind, however, was not on stalactites and stalagmites. Every time he closed his eyes, he saw Mary Elizabeth. When his eyes were open, he studied the fine features of Anica's face. Her mouth was slightly open as she looked about. Which of them was more beautiful? Joshua could not make a comparison. They were different girls, and each of them meant something different to him.

Anica's touch, her warmth, her affection, moved Joshua deeply. He adored her. He would love her unto his last breath, and if there was anything beyond death, he would love her for all eternity. Sitting with her here in this exotic place was wonderful. He loved to be near her. He loved holding her close. He never ceased to be amazed by her beauty. Her eyes, her ears, her silky brown hair, her mouth. Had he ever seen a prettier mouth? Yet her lips had never met his. It had not occurred to him that he might kiss her.

When he had been with Mary Elizabeth in the garden, he had kissed her, not just because he wanted to, but because the glow that surrounded her had drawn him into her, and he had surrendered to it without a thought. It was something that was meant to happen. He would love Mary Elizabeth for all of eternity, too. They were part of one another now; they had been so close that all of the borders that existed between them just melted away. Being apart from her now made him feel incomplete, yet he loved being here with Ani.

Joshua could not remember, but it was how he had felt when he would wonder at her in her crib. It was how he had felt when she was in diapers, happily chasing him around the house, waiting for him to do something funny so she would laugh. It was how he had felt when they sat facing one another in a wading pool, each of them joyfully slapping the water to keep each other wet. Jumping and rolling in a pile of leaves in the fall. Running to her when kindergarten let out and she came with Mom to pick him up. How had he ever let this go? What had happened to make him pull away?

Last night with Mary Elizabeth, the years of bitterness ended. It would not matter when he returned to Truman Jr. High and Jesse taunted him, or a teacher would scold him for daydreaming. No one else in the world would ever experience what he'd found with her. All he needed to do was remember the look in her beautiful green eyes, and the scolds and insults would bounce off of him like raindrops off an umbrella.

Yet his feelings for Anica had awakened before he met her. No, 'awakened' would not be right. He had never stopped loving her. He had stopped loving himself. When his body began to change, it became impossible for him to disregard her beauty, and he believed he had fallen in love with her because he needed to love someone, someone who might return his love. He instinctively knew that Anica had never stopped loving him, either. Now that he had truly fallen in love, he was able to sort his feelings out. He did not need to choose between Anica and Mary Elizabeth. He could love them both without reservation, because he loved them differently. And how fortunate could he be, that these two wonderful girls loved him?

Anica pointed out a rock formation where a group of three stalactites, nearly identical to one another, formed a perfect triangle as they passed under them. Joshua held his sister close and followed her gaze, rejoicing at the wonder in her eyes.

Grandma Aggie's funeral was held in the cathedral in downtown Cliffordsborough. Mom told him she wanted to get back on the road home when the service was over. Joshua's heart sank. It wasn't fair. He needed more time. He wanted forever.

Quite a few people were already seated in the pews when they arrived. Joshua looked around furtively for Mary Elizabeth, but he couldn't see her. He was starting to fret when he finally caught sight of her. She and her mother arrived with a tall man and two older boys. An usher seated them in a pew a few rows behind him. She wore a black skirt and leggings with a dark green sweater. Joshua tried to wave to her, but Aunt Alice scolded him to be more respectful.

He sat on the hard pew, trying not to fidget too obviously, but Aunt Alice poked his ribs anyway. Why couldn't he have sat next to Anica? The service was long, as many people wanted to stand up and say some words. The priest topped it off with a lengthy homily that made Joshua rethink his idea about wanting to be Catholic.

When the service finally ended, Joshua bolted from the pew to catch up with Mary Elizabeth.

"Joshua!" Aunt Alice snapped at him, rising to follow. The hell with Aunt Alice, he thought smugly, there's no way she can catch me. Mary Elizabeth was waiting – waiting for him – at the head of the steps leading down from the vestibule. He wanted to sweep her into his arms, to kiss her passionately, and never let her go again. But instead, all he could say was "Hi."

"Hi," she answered him. Their eyes met and the glow returned. A moment passed before she went to her mother.

"Mom? Can I talk with Joshua for a few minutes?"

Irene Connor regarded the two of them, aware that there was something between them.

"Of course, dear. We should stay and talk a while with the family, anyway."

Joshua's heart leapt when her parents and brothers turned to make their way towards a crowd of people gathered outside the church. Mary Elizabeth stood before him, looking so beautiful even dressed in something so plain. She approached him and, looking back to see if her family was watching, took his hands and quickly kissed him on the cheek. She motioned to a little shrine some distance from the side of the Cathedral. Holding his hand, she led him there.

They sat down on a small marble bench that reminded Joshua of the ones in the garden. He leaned forward to kiss her, but she hesitated. Joshua's heart grew troubled as she turned her head, but he saw that she was looking again to see if someone was watching.

When she was sure they were not, it was she who leaned into him, put her arms around his neck, and kissed him tenderly. All at once, everything was right with the world again.

They broke their embrace, but still sat close together, holding hands.

"Not really any place we can go from here," she told him. "I'm supposed to meet my family on the cathedral steps in half an hour."

They kissed again, and then just held each other for a long time. Half an hour, that was a lot of time, Joshua had thought, but it went by so quickly.

"We have to go now," Mary Elizabeth said, rising. Joshua stood up with her. He knew he was going to be in trouble when he connected with his own family again, but right now, he didn't care about anything but her.

"When, when can I see you again?"

Mary Elizabeth said, "How often do you get down here?" She said it in a way that let him know she already knew the answer. Tears welled up in Joshua's eyes.

"But I love you, Mary Elizabeth."

She approached to kiss him one more time. Joshua could not let her go, but he knew that he must.

"I love you too, Joshua. But we still have to go."

"So, so never?" Joshua could not stifle his sobs any longer.

She took his hands. "Never is a long time, Joshua. Don't ever say it, and don't ever think it."

"Joshua!" he heard his mother's voice shouting from the edge of the lawn where the shrine stood. "What do you mean, running off like that? We were worried sick. You are in so much..."

Agnes saw the tears in his eyes, Mary Elizabeth standing but a few inches next to him. Not speaking, he looked his mother straight in the eye and defiantly took her hand.

"Meet us at the car when you're ready, okay?" she said, the anger gone from her voice, and turned to go.

Joshua walked with Mary Elizabeth slowly, holding her hand, until they reached the steps of the church. In sight of her family, she gently let go of his hand. Joshua looked into her eyes. There were tears welling in them now.

She reached behind her neck to unclasp the silver chain with the little cross she always wore. She placed it in the palm of his hand and closed his fingers around it, now holding his hand in both of hers.

"Never is a long time." she said softly.

She turned to walk towards her family and did not look back.

Becky

Becky sat at her usual table with Natalie and Erin and Caitlin, delighted that a warm spring day had allowed her to go without leggings. Her short, pleated skirt had turned a lot of heads today.

The sad-eyed boy had been out of school on Friday, but he was there now, sitting alone, as usual, at the small table in the opposite corner of the cafeteria. He was not looking her way – had not since he seated himself. He hadn't touched his lunch, even though the bell would be ringing soon. Rather, he was looking down, turning something over in his hands. It looked like a thin silver chain with a pendant, maybe a cross. He glanced at the clock, and then held the silver chain close to his heart for a moment before dropping it into his shirt pocket. He took a sip of his soda and then a bite from his sandwich.

As she watched him now, Becky was intrigued, and to her surprise, a little hurt that he hadn't looked for her. He finally raised his head to look her way, now aware that she was looking at him. He glanced momentarily into her eyes and smiled just a little, before he returned to his lunch. *He never smiles*, she thought. He still appeared to be sadder than ever, but what had happened to his bashfulness?

When the bell rang, he left the cafeteria by the far door. She thought of following him for a moment, but the lunchroom was chaotic as the other students clamored to place their trays on the conveyor and get to their next class.

After school that day, Becky rose from the desk in her room, happy to be finished with her homework. She thought she might go out and hit some tennis balls against the garage before dinner. She put her books and papers into her backpack and set it on top of her bookcase. Of course – her bookcase! She retrieved a set of three thin paperbound volumes from the bottom shelf and found the one she wanted:

Lincolncrest Elementary School
2015-2016

Third grade, her first year in Glen Park. She thought back to her first day of school. A line of thunderstorms had rolled in, waking her before her alarm. The lawn of their new house was littered with hailstones when her mom pulled out of the garage to take her to school.

"What a terrible day!" Becky remarked, watching from the window of her mother's car as sheets of rain washed across the streets. "It never rained like this at home!"

"Rebecca," her mother said, "you are home. We talked about this."

They'd talked about it, but she'd had no say in it,

Becky thought despairingly. It would rain like this during the summer. In the fall, the leaves would change color, which she kind of looked forward to, but it would get colder, and in winter, there would be snow and ice and weeks of unrelenting cold. Her father took her skiing in the San Gabriels, and it was fun. But she was always happy when they were out of the mountains and she could ride the rest of the way home with the top of Dad's BMW convertible down, basking in the warm California sunshine.

Sunshine was nowhere in sight right now. This was not the way she had wanted to make her entrance at a brand new school. The dropoff lane at Lincolncrest Elementary School was backed up. She saw the children ahead of her running for the door with their backpacks held over their heads, or just walking quickly if they had umbrellas or raincoats. Becky carried an umbrella made of clear plastic that covered her like a dome, but she still did not like the idea of her new Nikes getting wet, especially with the new sparkle laces she'd just put in them.

Becky collapsed her umbrella and shook it once she was inside. Children were scurrying everywhere. Some had gathered in corners to mingle with their friends. Becky thought sadly of her friends in Brentwood Park mingling without her. She didn't know a soul here. She would have to change that quickly, she thought.

She'd been given a tour of Lincolncrest when her mother had enrolled her a few weeks ago, so she knew how to find her classroom, Room 136, Mrs. Marcus. Right turn, through the library, and right again. Her clothes were dry and her short blond hair was still neatly in place, held back from her face by a blue sparkle hairband. Her shoes were soaking wet, but not dirty. She wore white corduroy short shorts with frayed cuffs and a ribbed blue tank top. It felt a little cold to her, and she hoped that the building would get warmer when the sun returned.

She made her way through the foyer toward the entrance to the library. Two boys crossed ahead of her and collided when they both jerked their heads her way. Becky smiled at them as she passed. Some things hadn't changed, she thought. The amusement lifted her mood as she made her way to Room 136.

She found a peg with her name under it on the wall outside the classroom, and she hung her umbrella there. Mrs. Marcus stood outside the door, greeting each pupil as they entered. When Becky stopped to introduce herself, Mrs. Marcus was expecting her.

"Oh, you must be Rebecca Lindstrom! Welcome to Lincolncrest Elementary. You're going to have a great year here, Rebecca."

"Thank you," Becky said insincerely, thinking of the snow and ice ahead. "And it's Becky. Everyone calls me Becky," she continued graciously. Most of her class were already in their seats. She looked around to find the card with her name. There! She would sit at a table with two girls named Natalie Winthrop and Caitlin Vincelli, and a boy named Keith Weber. She took her seat and slid her sparkle blue backpack underneath her chair. The two girls promptly introduced themselves and complimented her clothes and her hair. Keith Weber sat in his chair looking a little shaken. Becky introduced herself to him, and he said hello, but his hand was shaky when she shook it. The two girls happily chatted and gossiped with her until the bell rang.

All the seats save one were filled. Mrs. Marcus started calling out names for attendance. When she was up through the Ks, a boy shambled in. He was soaked from head to toe.

"Joshua," she said curtly, "please go to the boys' room and dry yourself off as best you can. And school starts at 8:10 this year, same as last year." Many around the classroom chuckled as Joshua left the room. Mrs. Marcus was finished with attendance when he returned. He glanced around the room trying to find his seat, but he didn't see a card with his name on it. Mrs. Marcus frowned and announced,

"Who has Joshua's name card? Jesse?" A few chuckles broke out again. A husky boy at the table in front of Becky's reached into his drawer and replaced the card on the table, in front of the empty chair.

160

Joshua unhappily took his seat while the other boy smirked.

Oh, my God, that was mean, Becky thought to herself angrily. Mrs. Marcus stood at the front of the room to commence with the morning announcements.

"Jesse, please see me at recess," she scowled at the mean kid at the table in front of hers. Now smiling, she said,

"Class, we have a new student at Lincolncrest this year! Rebecca, would you like to come up and introduce yourself?"

"It's Becky," she repeated as she stood at the front of the room. "Hi, my name is Becky Lindstrom, and my family just moved here from Brentwood Park, California. My father is a lawyer, and my mom is out trying to find things for our new house. I love cats, and I like to ski and play tennis," she continued, and then, pointedly, "And I really, really hate mean people!"

All eyes in the room were on her. This didn't make Becky nervous at all. She'd already made two friends and it wasn't quite 8:30. The girls looked her up and down, approving of her choice of clothes. The boys gazed at her, wide-eyed and slackjawed. She shot the mean kid a frown, which caused him to sheepishly lower his head. The boy who'd come in late – he gazed at her, too, but not quite like the others did. There was a look of wonder on his face that Becky found flattering. She tried to smile at him, but he averted his

161

eyes when he saw she was looking his way.

Becky returned to her seat. The boy with the wet clothes took out his backpack and tried to find a spiral notebook that hadn't gotten wet in the rain. The rest of the day, he said nothing and hurried towards the exit when the last bell rang.

I miss California, Becky lamented.

Becky thumbed through the yearbook to find Mrs. Marcus's class. There! His picture was right next to hers. He did not smile, but he looked so cute, adorable even, in his white shirt and red tie.

Becky slapped her forehead. "Joshua! Of course, Joshua Miller!" She said, out loud. Then,

"You're still cute, Joshua Miller, but you still don't smile. Whatever can we do about that?"

She returned the yearbooks to her bookcase and fetched her racket from the closet. Entering her back yard through the patio door, she was so happy it was finally spring.

162

Joshua

Joshua took his seat for 9th period study hall. He ran his hand over the silver chain in his pocket through the fabric of his shirt. He dare not take it out, or Mrs. Addison would surely see and confiscate it.

He opened his math workbook and thumbed to a blank page in his spiral. He copied the first problem onto his paper and stared at the blank space below. The problem was to add two mixed numbers with fractions that had different denominators. He thumbed back through his spiral a couple of pages and tried to make sense of the notes he'd scrawled in third period. He had managed to copy a problem from the board that looked something like the one from his workbook, but he could not remember what Mrs. Simmons did to get from one step to the next.

Mrs. Addison was seated at her desk, grading a quiz she had given to her regular students. Joshua raised his hand. She glanced at him, then went back to her work. Joshua kept his hand in the air. After a minute, she looked up at him again, wearing a scowl.

"Joshua, you had time to go to the bathroom before the bell. Now you're just going to have to wait until the period is over." She sounded irritated. Joshua lowered his hand and decided he would not try to ask Mrs. Addison for help again.

He felt for the silver chain again. I'm not a loser, he

thought. He looked back down at his notebook to the problem he'd copied from the board. He had been so intent on copying it down right that he could not comprehend what Mrs. Simmons did to get from one step to the next. What did she do? Or what could she have done? He returned to the problem from his workbook. He racked his brain. Some of it was familiar to him, so he worked on those parts.

He remembered how to add the fractions. He started with those. He just added the result to the sum of the whole numbers and wrote that down as the answer. He had no idea whether or not he had done anything right, but at least he did something instead of scrawling gibberish to make it look like he was working.

The bell rang. It had taken him the entire period to do one problem. He lined up with the other kids waiting for Mrs. Addison to dismiss them one by one. When he got to the door, he turned to her and said, quietly, "I didn't have to go."

He left the room and started down the hall towards room 187C, his math classroom. Mrs. Simmons was at her desk, looking through the homework she assigned on Friday, when Joshua was out. He entered the classroom and she looked up at him.

"Joshua, what brings you here? I don't think you've ever come to see me after school when I didn't tell you to."

Joshua took out his notebook and showed her the problem he did in study hall.

"I wrote down what you did in class, but I couldn't remember how you did it," he explained. "I tried to do it this way, but I think it's wrong. Can you show me again?"

Mrs. Simmons looked at his work.

"Why do you think it's wrong?" she asked him.

"I don't know what I'm doing. It was just something to try. I really wanted to do the problem, but I didn't know how. I just didn't want to give up again."

Mrs. Simmons regarded him earnestly.

"Joshua, this is almost the right answer. You just need to reduce this last fraction here. Otherwise, you didn't make any mistakes. Can I see how you did the rest of them?"

Joshua felt good about doing something right, but he wasn't happy that it took him so long.

"I just did that one. It took me the whole period to figure it out."

"Do you have something you have to do now?" she asked.

"No. I just want to be home when my sister gets home from her piano lesson. That won't be until 5 or so."

Mrs. Simmons smiled at him. She took a pen and drew lines through the even numbered problems on the assigned page in his workbook.

"Let's just forget about these, okay? Now, why don't you sit down and get started on number three. Do it the way you did the first one. I'll help you if you get stuck."

Joshua started work on the problem. Now that he knew the method he tried in study hall was all right, it took him only a few minutes. Mrs. Simmons said it was right. He asked her if he could stay and do some more of them. By 4:00, he finished all of the ones Mrs. Simmons told him he had to do.

She took his paper and reached into her drawer, where she kept a rubber stamp with a little star on it. She stamped his paper and put it in a folder in her file drawer. Joshua knew about the stars, but he'd never gotten one before.

"Now go home and see your sister," she said, with a smile. "And Joshua? I'm here after school every day."

Joshua sat in the living room trying to read some papers that were handed out in his social studies class. Mom and Anica came in through the kitchen. They said hello to Joshua, then Mom went to the kitchen to start dinner. Anica sat down at her piano and spread out some sheet music she brought home from her lesson. Joshua asked her,

"Ani? When you're done with practice, do you think we can work on my handwriting some more? And maybe help me with this reading? There are some

166

words I don't know."

Anica stood up and smiled at her brother.
"Mozart can wait," she said.

Agnes

Agnes and her children no longer attended church on Sunday. John had started going erratically, and had then stopped altogether, claiming that the demands of his business made it impossible. Agnes was puzzled and skeptical, as John had always told her it was against the scriptures to toil on the Sabbath. But then, John was becoming more and more erratic in everything. He went to his office every day now, often staying very late, and he would collapse into bed without a word to her.

She was worried. It began around the time they returned from Anica's piano recital. Joshua's conduct at home and in school was improving. Joshua had started doing his chores regularly, and he even started picking up his room, with a little help from his sister. The disturbing letters and voicemails from his school had stopped. Agnes was proud of her son for the effort he was making, but John paid scant attention to it. Fortunately for Joshua, John was gone most of the time now.

John also started to take an interest in Anica, but it was not something either Agnes or her daughter welcomed. He did not concern himself with her excellent grades or her prowess at the piano and on the balance beam. He began to take more notice of her appearance. Anica was always a strikingly pretty girl, and her manners of dress and grooming were impeccable and modest. She was, however, entering puberty and it was starting to show. Agnes would sometimes catch John looking at his daughter in a peculiar way. When she talked to him about it, he started going on about how there would soon be boys calling on her at the house and he would have to chase them away.

Then there were the little things. He stopped washing his car. He no longer shined his shoes. These were things that had been a ritual to him. He'd put on a tie with a spot on it the other day. He no longer read the Sunday paper.

Her first real indication that something was terribly wrong was when he came home close to midnight one night, clearly drunk, almost staggering. She had never known him to take a drink.

"John, why have you been drinking? I've never seen you like this before."

John began to cry. She had never known him to cry, either.

"I lost Good News today."

Good News was a chain of stores that sold Christian books and merchandise. The management had purchased group term life insurance from him, and it provided him with a steady stream of revenue. It was John's biggest account.

"I'm sorry, Agnes. I won't do it again." Agnes had

never known him to apologize, either.

He seemed better for a few days. He came home for dinner on Friday. Come Sunday, he took the family to church after weeks of skipping services. The following week, however, his erratic behavior returned. She thought she could smell liquor on his breath sometimes, but he did not appear to be drunk. She let it go. She remembered that her father sometimes took a drink or two when he'd had a stressful day at work. John was obviously under stress.

She was concerned for him, and it hurt her to see that he was clearly in pain. She could admit to herself that she and her husband had not been close for quite some time. She wanted him to work through his problems. When she and John were first married, they were so much closer, and she was sometimes able to get John to open up to her. He was outwardly strong and confident, but she knew even then that he held a great deal of pain inside of himself. He had told her of the abuse he'd received at the hands of his father, of how that had led to his estrangement from his mother, but she knew she hadn't heard all of it. It went on for most of John's childhood and adolescence, and ended only when his father died suddenly. Even if John were far more open with her, she didn't think he could have told her all of it.

Could she still be there for him? Could she get him to open up to her again, at least just a little, so she could know more of what he was going through? Could she convince him it was something they could face together? She feared it was too late, and she grew increasingly concerned for the children, Anica in particular. It troubled her terribly, and she was afraid.

Agnes and the children still visited her mother every Sunday. Her brother Alan had come today with his brood, and the adults stayed inside talking around the kitchen table while the children went outside to play.

"Honestly, Alan, I don't know," Agnes explained. "He has everything sent to his office – the bank statements, the credit cards, the mortgage statements, the car payments, and the utilities. I don't know how much we have or how much we owe! One of the credit cards was declined at Target last week, but the other one went through, thank God. Then there's the drinking and the way he's been around the children. His birthday was four weeks ago, and he hasn't opened his presents."

"Agnes, dear, just find out how much you owe and let me pay it off," her mother said. "Lord knows, your father left us enough!"

"That's not what Dad wanted, Mother."

"Well, he didn't want his daughter and his grandchildren living on the streets, either!"

"You can go to your bank and get them to print off a statement for you," Alan explained. "And you can call the numbers on the back of your cards to find out what your balance is. Same thing with the mortgage company and the bank that holds the titles on your cars."

"Just let me pay it off, Alan."

Alan Adler fished around in his wallet until he found a business card. It was from a law firm in the city. He stood up on his prosthetic leg and crossed to her side of the table to give it to her.

"Agnes, I want you to call this guy. He does mainly corporate law, but I've known him for a long time, and he's good, trustworthy. Some of the people in his firm handle domestic relations."

Agnes started to cry.

"I just don't know if it's come to that, Alan. Can't you talk to him? He's your friend. The two of you used to talk for hours."

"Agnes," Alan told her, "I like John. It's hard not to. He's tough, he's smart, and he's strong. But I've seen this before. The things that made him strong are eating him up on the inside."

"He won't talk to me Alan. I can barely get a word out of him about the agency and he used to talk about it all the time. He never wanted to talk about his life in Tennessee. He got upset if I even brought it up. But now, he doesn't want to talk about anything, not his job, his church, the children, anything."

Her brother's manner became grave. He pulled his

172

chair from the other side of the table and sat down close to her.

"I knew this guy named MacGregor when I was in Afghanistan. He was an E-7, fifteen years in, Desert Storm, Tora Bora, tough as they come. A man you want to have watching your back in a fight.

"One day, he just up and stopped talking to anybody. He would answer you if you spoke to him, but the rest of the time, he started keeping to himself. Wasn't like him. He was vulgar, liked to crack jokes, liked to mess around with you. We all liked him. We played poker with this guy all the time, but that stopped, too. He just sat on his bunk, cleaning his guns and sharpening his knife. Or he would just lie there, staring at the ceiling.

"We were stationed at an outpost a couple hundred clicks north of Kandahar. Got some intel from the locals about a Taliban encampment in the hills outside their village. Our C.O. ordered four of us to check it out. MacGregor took point. When we got to the place where the Taliban were holed up, there must have been thirty of them. They had AKs, mortars, and RPGs. We were supposed to fall back, report, and wait for orders. Instead, MacGregor just walked into the camp and started shooting. He took out two or three of them, then the rest of them cut him to ribbons, kept shooting him after he was dead. Never saw something that awful, not even when I lost my leg. We had to

173

hightail it back to our Humvee and get out of there before they spotted us.

"Nobody knew what made him snap. We knew he enlisted on his eighteenth birthday. Guys who do that are usually running from something. Your husband, John, he's starting to act like MacGregor. Agnes, when a man like that breaks, he shatters. If you can't get him to seek help, then you'd best get out of the way."

John

9:40 PM, John thought. He'd best be getting home.

Not that he had been particularly busy. He'd spoken with his last client more than 2 hours ago. He'd passed the time since going through the ledger, occasionally glancing at the large portrait of Jesus on his wall, praying He could somehow make the numbers look better than the last time he went over them.

Then there was the stack of memoranda on his desk. The Christian Guaranty Life Insurance Company was not doing well. In trouble with regulators in two of the nineteen southern and midwestern states where they did business, they were cutting expenses in an effort to bring their policy reserves in line with state regulations. Underproducing agencies were being systematically cut loose. The Miller Insurance Agency had sold exactly six middling policies in as many weeks. The commissions from those wouldn't go far, and the lack of sales would not go unnoticed by the home office.

John was alone. The other desks in the office stood bare, abandoned. One by one, the three other agents who worked with him had left to find business elsewhere. He'd let his secretary go months ago. He'd cut expenses in every way he could, but he was still operating in the red. He'd kept his family afloat by depending on Agnes's salary, making minimum payments on their credit cards, and systematically selling off assets that would soon run out if business didn't pick up. He couldn't tell Agnes any of it, or she'd go running to his mother-in-law who could buy and sell him a hundred times over.

The thought galled him. If the old battleaxe would just die, his family would be okay and he might be able to get his business back on its feet. But then, they might as well call it the Adler Insurance Agency. That would strip him of whatever was left of his pride, so the thought of that galled him too.

John slammed the ledger shut angrily. What business did the government have, scrutinizing the books and sales practices of a company that was doing God's work? And what business did that company have, threatening to close the agency of a man who had brought them so many clients, so much business? The past two years had been lean, but he had done so well up to then. It was a sin!

"Sin." John muttered aloud. "Sin everywhere!"

Even under his own roof, John thought bitterly. Agnes had started taking exercise classes at the YMCA. She took smaller portions at dinner and gave up desserts. She'd been getting her hair done. Painting her nails. She'd let herself go after their daughter was born, but lately she was getting less heavy and had been buying some new clothes. She loved the compliments she got on the new dress she wore on

Easter. Women, all the same, he thought. The sin of vanity!

And that good-for-nothing son of his! Never picking up after himself, dawdling through his chores, picking at the food the Good Lord provided. Always daydreaming, never planting his feet on the ground. Fidgeting in their pew in church, stumbling over the words when reciting the congregational prayers. John sometimes wondered if he was even his son. Had Agnes stepped out on him when she was still attractive, maybe with that man she worked for at the construction company? What did she actually do there?

That girl, that girl, she was becoming a problem, too. Money for piano lessons. Money for gymnastics classes. Money to replace clothes she had outgrown in less than a year. Dear Lord, he thought to himself, she was ruining him. He'd even had to pay for that motel room after the concert Agnes had insisted he attend. What did the fabric for that dress Agnes made for her cost? The long, black satin dress she'd worn, shimmering in the footlights, seated at the big Steinway piano in the college auditorium in view of everybody. He'd distinctly heard some wretched man a couple of seats down from him whispering to his wife,

"She's going to break a lot of hearts, that one!"

And *deliver me from evil, O Lord*, the changes had begun, he thought bitterly. Agnes had brought home a

Marshall's bag full of girl's underwear last week. When he looked inside, he'd found bras! Little bras with tiny flower prints on them! He snapped at Agnes,

"What's the meaning of this? What are these doing in here?"

Agnes snapped back at him. "The girl is ten years old, John. Now those are training bras, she can't get by with just undershirts and camis any more. And you should know better than to be going through her underwear, John Miller! There are things a girl's entitled to keep to herself, whether you're her father or not."

Soon there would be boys coming around. Only interested in one thing, the lot of them! Black satin, he thought to himself again. That neckline, it almost showed her collarbone, and the string of pearls around her neck! Pearls! They belonged to Agnes's mother, but the way they'd looked on her ... no wonder that shameless, leering man down the row was talking dirty about her. Thank the Lord she would already be in bed when he got home. In bed, just down the hall from him. John dug his nails into his palms until they hurt, trying to make the sinful feeling pass.

"Sin!" the words of his father, thundering from his pulpit, rang in John's ears. "This world, this wretched world, drowning in sin! But! But, Heavenly Father, all across our land, Christians are answering Your call.

We shall rise up to vanquish the demons Satan has let loose on the world! I pray thee, O Lord, let us be Your army of righteousness! The end times are upon us! Send Thy Holy Wrath down upon the sinners, that they be cast into the lake of fire!"

Around the congregation, he heard scattered cries of "Hallelujah! Amen! Praise be! Bless you, Reverend John!"

John Miller the younger shrank in his pew, knowing that he sinned, casting his seed into the filth. Filth. Sin. And unable to stop, surely Satan had taken possession of him. He must fight him, cast him out! But the girls, the girls from his school, the ones seated here in the congregation – he couldn't stop thinking about them. Eve's temptation! He was unable to resist it despite the teachings of the Scriptures and his constant fear of the Reverend John Miller's heavy leather belt.

John grew up in Arlo, Tennessee, a small farming town 40 miles from Knoxville. His father, John the elder, was the minister of a small Pentecostal church on the edge of town. Reverend John, as everyone called him, was a tall, gaunt man with a powerful voice and piercing dark eyes. He had been fifty-three years old when John the younger was born on April 16, 1969.

John's mother, Constance Anne Miller, Reverend John's second wife, was considerably younger. She was a small woman who'd been born on a farm outside Arlo and seldom ventured anywhere else. Her family had been members of the congregation of the Arlo Pentecostal Church since she was born, and every Sunday she hung on his every word, believing him to be the voice of God Himself.

Constance Anne was nineteen when Reverend John's first wife died, leaving him childless. People from all over the valley crowded into his church to pay their respects. Reverend John had taken his place at the pulpit, and had preached that this was not a time for grief, but for rejoicing that God had so loved her that he called her home early. So brave and resolute he had been, thought Constance, preaching the Gospel to his flock even as his wife's body lay in state before the altar.

Constance Anne always sat in the front row of the church. Her eyes never left Reverend John as he preached. In time, some six months after the passage of his wife, he took a fancy to her. Not long after that, they married and she bore him a son. They named him John, not for himself, John the elder had explained, but for John the Divine, author of the Book of Revelations, foreteller of the End Times which must surely be upon us.

Life was hard in Arlo. The recessions of the 1970s had hit rural Tennessee particularly hard. Like most of the townspeople, the Millers were poor. The

Pentecostal sect that had ordained John the elder
consisted of some 50 churches scattered in little towns
like Arlo throughout Tennessee, Kentucky, and north
Georgia. They paid him a small salary and allowed
him to set aside a portion of the collection plate for his
own expenses. It was barely enough to get by. John
and his family lived in the 70-year-old rectory adjacent
to the church. It was a little house with a kitchen, a
common room, and two tiny bedrooms, the lesser of
which became John the younger's room as he grew
older. There was a hand pump above the kitchen sink
and an outhouse out back. A wood burning stove in the
common room was the only source of heat in the
winter. The roof leaked when it rained, and a draft
blew through the house when it was windy. Thanks to
the church, they had electricity that powered the lights
and a refrigerator, but the wiring was old and fuses
blew constantly. There was a telephone in the church
office. Their only luxury was an old table radio that
was always tuned to a Gospel station in Knoxville.

A rickety barn even older than the house stood in
the fields behind the rectory and the church. The
church owned a few acres of land where the Millers
grew vegetables, berries, apples, and a few rows of
corn for the family to eat and to can for the winter.
Constance Anne's father would bring his tractor to
help with the spring tilling. Many of the congregation
would turn out in the fall to help with the harvest and

the canning. What the Millers did not need for themselves, they gave to the poorest members of the church.

When John the younger was six years old, his father put him to work sweeping the floors of the church, polishing the candlesticks, and doing odd jobs around the house. If his father was not satisfied with the work, he would make him start over until he got it right.

John the elder's temper was as fiery as his sermons. Once, on a chilly November day, John forgot to fill the wood basket for the stove. His father commanded him to follow him outdoors to the woodpile, where he made him drop his trousers and beat him soundly on his buttocks and legs with his belt.

John soon learned to remember all of his chores and to do them well and quickly, but the beatings continued. Almost anything could set his father off. Stumbling over a Bible verse when he was called upon to read. Hanging up his coat with acorns in its pockets. Sitting down at the table with dirt behind his ears.

His father preached constantly about sin, about how all the peoples of the earth were sinners whose souls hung in a precarious balance between salvation and perdition, awaiting God's judgment. In time, John grew to accept the beatings as God's punishment for his sins, although he wasn't always sure what he had sinned about.

When John entered puberty, he had no idea what was happening to him. He took an interest in the girls at the tiny town's K-8 school, and at night, he could not stop thinking about them. He could not pray it away. In time, as all boys do, he discovered something that he was certain was a mortal sin and that God would strike him down in his bed if he did not find a way to stop it. One evening, his father commanded him to read from Genesis 38:

> *And Onan knew that the seed should not be his; and it came to pass, when he went in unto his brother's wife, that he spilled it on the ground, lest that he should give seed to his brother.*
>
> *And the thing which he did displeased the Lord: wherefore he slew him also.*

This, of course, had not been a coincidence. It mortified John, confirming his worst fears. Yet, he could not stop, and each night after he was through, he waited for God to slay him.

Although John was outwardly obedient, there was a part of him inside that remained defiant. As he awaited his judgment, he thought:

It can't be worse than my father's belt.

When John was fifteen, his chores had become more numerous, so much so that it was hard for him to

183

keep up with his studies. John did very well in school. He was bright enough to know that getting an education would be his way out of Arlo and its poverty. The long bus ride to and from the high school in the county seat forced him to leave his chores in the morning and delay them in the afternoon. He had to work past dark to keep up, and continue after dinner.

He would often lie on the floor of his room late at night, doing his lessons by the light of a coal oil lantern, a blanket stuffed under the crack in his door lest his father discover he was not sleeping. When his lessons were done, he turned to the books he'd checked out of the library at school.

Between his chores and his studies, John was always short on sleep. He slept on the bus on the way to and from school. Early in his first year in high school, some older boys took some amusement in this. They made fun of him as he slept, getting a laugh out of the other teens riding the bus with them. One morning, as they left the bus, the boys continued making fun of John. He ignored them and started to make his way to class. It escalated. The boys followed him, continuing their taunts and insults. John did nothing until one of them punched him in the shoulder.

John turned to the boy abruptly, a scowl of rage on his face. When the boy tried to push him to the ground, John easily sidestepped him and hurled him to the ground instead. John let him get up and waited for the

184

punch. He caught the boy's hand in his and threw a haymaker of his own into his nose, and he fell to the ground bleeding. He might have gotten up, but he didn't. Instead, he held out his hand in a gesture that meant "no more."

By this time, a teacher had come to break up the fight. John desisted immediately, backing away and bowing his head. The teacher hauled both of them into the principal's office. When the principal asked them which of them had started it, neither of them said anything. Neither did any of the other kids who'd witnessed the altercation.

The principal made calls to the parents. John the elder answered at the church office and listened carefully to what the principal told him. When John got off the bus that day, his father waited for him.

The beating John got was lighter than usual, and his father made no more of it for the rest of the day. His father was clearly more tolerant of John's dealings with boys than he was of his interest in girls.

At age fourteen, John matched his father in height and outweighed him by thirty pounds of lean muscle. At any time, and for some time now, he could have turned to his father the way he'd turned to the bully from the bus and thrown him to the ground like a scarecrow. He did not. He feared his father as much as he feared God himself. But the boys on the bus never taunted him again, nor did anyone else.

Even the beatings got lighter, but they also got more unpredictable, more about keeping him in line than about punishing him for any particular thing. Even when his father was teaching him how to drive, he was not punished for his mistakes, just made to repeat whatever he'd done wrong. John might have taken some encouragement from this, but by now, his fear of his father was so complete there was no room for reason.

On an oppressively hot summer's day in 1985, John accompanied his father to Perkins' Feed and Hardware in the ancient GMC pickup the church had bought for him. Outside the store were Arlo's only gas pumps. Just inside the door was an area where people could buy snacks and cold drinks. John stayed outside to gas up the truck while his father went in to buy a dozen rolls of tar paper and two pounds of roofing nails to patch the roof of the rectory.

A big, shiny, new Oldsmobile sedan pulled into the parking lot. It had Ohio plates and a decal from a dealership in Cincinnati. Tourists, John surmised. Arlo didn't get many of them, but sometimes they came to visit a historical site in town, a carefully restored and preserved cottage that had been a waystop on the Underground Railroad. The front doors opened. A man and a woman got out and entered the store. John went back about his business, wanting no truck with strangers.

186

Andie and Amy craned their necks to look out the back window at the tall boy filling up the tank of the old pickup.

"He's a hunk!" Andie exclaimed.

"He's a hick!" Her fraternal twin sister said.

"Come on, let's go talk to him!"

"Dad said to stay in the car. The motor's running."

"Just for a minute. It'll be fun. I'll bet he talks with a drawl. I want to hear him talk."

Amy sighed at her sister, then she took the tourist's guide from the front seat and reached for the door handle.

John wiped his brow on his shirt after he hung the nozzle back on the gas pump. He glanced over at the big, flashy car parked a few feet away. The back doors opened. Two girls in their middle teens emerged. John had never seen girls such as these before. They were beautiful. They had long, shiny hair that hung to the middle of their backs. They wore cutoff blue jeans so short that the pockets protruded from beneath the frayed, faded denim. And so tight! Their shirts were sleeveless, cropped just below the ribs. John could clearly see their navels. He had never before seen a girl's navel, and it excited him greatly.

One of the girls was carrying a book he'd seen before, a catalogue of historical sites throughout Tennessee. They both approached him. John was at once frightened and overwhelmed by their beauty.

187

When they drew near to him, one of the girls smiled and pointed to a picture of Arlo's Civil War house, saying,

"Hi! Excuse me, do you know where this is?"

John pointed in the direction of the house and tried to stammer some directions. At that moment, his father emerged from the store, carrying a box of nails and a slip of paper to give to the boys who would load the tar paper into the truck.

"Johnny!" his father thundered angrily, "Go back and help the Perkins boys with the tar paper!"

To the startled girls, he snapped, "You two, y'all go back to your car and cover yourselves up! This is a God-fearin' town, we don't need no big city girls galavantin' around here half naked!"

The terrified girls ran back to the car and disappeared into the back seat. When their parents returned to the car, John the elder saw one of the girls pointing at him, and a moment later, the big car sped away straight out of town.

On the way back to the rectory, John the elder did not speak to his son, did not even look at him. The scowl he wore on his face made John tremble. When his father stopped the truck, John went immediately to the woodpile beside the house to receive his father's wrath.

"Whores! Trollops! The devil's temptation!" he roared as he removed his belt. "I'm a goin' to take your

188

hide off this time, boy. That'll get the devil out of ye!"

John the elder beat his son until the leather of his belt tore his flesh. Even as blood ran down his legs, he continued until John could no longer hold himself up and collapsed on the ground. He continued to beat him on his arms and shoulders, tearing his shirt. Finally, his mother emerged from the house to plead with her husband that the boy had had enough.

"Silence, woman!" he snapped at her, "Satan done took possession of this boy today! I'm a-doin' the Lord's work here!" Constance Anne dropped to her knees, wailing. Even the Reverend John Miller could not resist his wife's streaming tears.

In a lower, but still angry voice, he told John,

"Ye'll be sleepin' in the barn tonight, and ye ain't gettin' no supper. And mark my words, yo' mama won't save you from the whuppin' you gonna get if I ever see you talkin' to any of them girls again. Any of 'em! Girls, all o' them, cursed for all time for bringin' sin into this world."

The night was no cooler than the day. John lay on his side on a pile of straw, unable to find a position that did not hurt. Sweat stung his undressed wounds. He decided the time had come for him to leave this place. He would stow away in one of the big trucks that brought merchandise to Perkins' Feed and Hardware. He didn't care where it was headed, as long as it was away from Arlo and this man who would

189

surely beat him to death if he stayed.

A scream pierced the heavy night air, his mother's scream. He feared his father was taking his hand to her for intervening on his behalf today, but then he heard the screen door bang and the sound of his mother's footsteps running toward the barn. He struggled to get up as she entered.

"Johnny! Johnny! Somethin' done happened to your father!" He had never seen his mother so frantic before. As quickly as he could manage, he limped after her back to the rectory. His father was sprawled motionless in the house's only upholstered chair, arms out to his side, his head back, eyes open but seeming to stare at the ceiling. The yellow notepad he used to compose his sermons lay on the floor beside him, as did the thick, indexed King James Bible he used.

It took nearly half an hour for paramedics to arrive from the county seat 20 miles distant. At 11:44 PM on July 8th, 1985, the Reverend John Miller was pronounced dead from cardiac arrest.

The Pentecostals dispatched a minister to preside over his funeral. An elder of Reverend John's flock delivered the eulogy, praising him as the finest of God's servants he had ever known. John, as yet unable to sit down, stood or knelt throughout the ceremony. When the pallbearers took Reverend John's coffin, John's tiny mother had to help him walk the short distance from the sanctuary to the small graveyard behind the church. The Reverend John Miller was laid to rest in a row set aside at the rear of the graveyard, joining the other former pastors of the Arlo Pentecostal Church.

As was custom, John followed his mother in tossing a handful of dirt atop his father's coffin. When no one was watching, he spat in the palm of his hand before clutching the dirt he threw.

John and his mother soon had to vacate the rectory when a new pastor was appointed to replace his father. They moved in with Constance Anne's parents on their farm a few miles from the town. John found life there to be little better than he'd had in Arlo. His grandfather woke him early in the morning to help with the milking. He toiled in the fields from sunup to sundown, which gave him blisters that turned to thick calluses. When his work was finally done, he would eat dinner with his mother and his grandparents, then collapse into a lumpy bed in a room as tiny as the one he'd had at the rectory. There he would sleep until it was time to get up and do it all over again.

His only relief came on Sundays, when his grandparents did not work him. Like his father, they did not toil on the Sabbath, but it also meant that the four of them would pile into his grandfather's truck and drive into Arlo to attend church – the same church where his father had preached. Ascending the steps into the sanctuary, John's memories of the years he had spent picking up trash and sweeping the floors flooded back to him. They sat in the front row, as his mother and grandparents always had. Old Mrs. Granger banged out the same hymns on the same out-of-tune upright piano in the corner. The faces in the congregation were all familiar to him.

The new pastor was a pudgy man with a balding scalp and rimless bifocal glasses. John scarcely listened to him as he droned through his dull, hollow sermon. It maddened John to think of how his father had stood at that pulpit for so many years, mesmerizing his congregation with the fiery crescendos of his preaching, the dramatic gestures of his hands, and his piercing black eyes. Compared to Reverend John, this man might as well have been the man on the morning radio, unenthusiastically reading the farm report.

The worst of it came when services ended. John's grandparents, his mother, and even John himself were treated as elders of the church. They spent a great deal of time standing in the foyer or on the steps, glad-handing and chatting with the congregation.

Conversation would invariably turn to his father; many in the church were unhappy with the new pastor and would reminisce about Reverend John's gift for oratory. John listened patiently as they continued to express their condolences for his loss.

When the crowd thinned out, his mother and he

would make their weekly pilgrimage to his father's grave. Constance Anne frequently wept there, prayed on her knees at his headstone, beseeching The Almighty to keep and care for his soul until the day when the souls of the righteous would be resurrected. John stood by respectfully, keeping silent, but in his thoughts, he mused,

Six feet under. Six feet closer to Hell.

When they returned to the farm after church, John retired to his room. He read from the few books he'd had at the rectory and what little he could find in his grandparents' home. He read from current and past issues of The Old Farmer's Almanac, painstakingly poring over the numbers and calculations there. He collected discarded magazines and catalogs from neighboring farms. When he could get his hands on a newspaper, he would read it through the last page, intent on learning as much as he could about the world outside of Arlo.

John desperately wanted to return to school in the fall, but his grandfather told him he would be too busy with the harvest then. He sank into an angry despair, as his studies had been the only good thing in his life. Each morning he would watch for the yellow school bus that took the other young people from Arlo and the surrounding farms to the high school in the county seat.

One October morning, he dropped his rake and ran

193

to hail the driver in front of his grandparents' farmhouse, stopping briefly to retrieve a feed sack containing some of his clothes and his Sunday shoes from under the front porch. The driver recognized him and stopped to pick him up. Without books or pencils, John boarded the bus, his overalls filthy from toiling in the dirt, and rode it to the county seat.

The doors of the high school beckoned, but this was not his destination. In the pocket of his dirty overalls was a wad of crumpled dollar bills he had taken from his grandmother's butter and egg money over a period of weeks. Taken, not stolen, he told himself. He had milked the cows for the butter. He had cleaned the chicken coop where she gathered her eggs. He did twice the work his grandfather did, all for some food and a lumpy bed to sleep in.

He walked to the Greyhound station in the center of town, and one by one counted out the nineteen dollars he needed for a ticket to Memphis.

John washed his clothes in a coin-op laundromat. He washed up in public toilets and slept in thickets and under bridges until he found an encampment where day laborers gathered, looking to pick up whatever work they could find. Years of hard living had made John Miller a strapping young man who looked older than his sixteen years. He found work easily and earned enough money to rent a room at the YMCA. The work became steadier, and he was eventually

194

hired on by a man who owned a small construction company. The money was good enough for him to move out of the Y into a rooming house near the center of town.

In time, he sent a short letter to his mother. He did not give her a return address, so she could not write back or send someone to look for him. He told her he was all right, that he had a job and a place to stay, and that she should not worry about him. At the same time, he mailed an envelope containing fifty-three dollars in cash to his grandmother, the amount he had taken to make his escape. He owed them no more. His grandparents were as hard and cold as the winter's ice. His mother had stood by for ten years as his father lashed away his childhood, his dignity, and his self-worth, intervening only after he had been beaten half to death.

John purchased a Bible soon after he'd gotten a foothold on life in Memphis, and read from it nightly. It was the first Bible he ever owned. When he was growing up in the rectory, he read from his father's Bible, and only the passages John the elder wanted him to read.

To be sure, John knew enough of the stories. He sat in the front row with his mother and grandparents every Sunday to hear his father preach. The church was always full; people came from as far away as Knoxville to hear the fabled Reverend John. Like all of the congregation, John listened to every word, every inflection, every subtle change in cadence. His father had a gift that came to him from above. John could not understand how the man could be so on fire with The Holy Spirit when he stood at his pulpit, and so rattlesnake mean the rest of the time. Was that the price of his gift? If so, it was John the younger who had paid it.

John began reading his Bible at Genesis 1 and continued through the Revelations 22. When he was finished, he would start over. Whenever he came across a passage his father had read from the pulpit, or had commanded him to recite beside his chair, he could hear his voice in his head. But as he read those same passages in context, he discovered new meanings to them that made him hate his father even more. John the elder had a Bible verse at the ready any time he did anything mean and coldhearted. Even as his hatred of his father grew, his reverence for the Scriptures grew deeper.

He found a suit and tie at a secondhand store, and he began to attend services at a Baptist church near the rooming house where he lived. He made friends there, and there were girls. He fancied one of them, a slender, pretty girl around sixteen years old named Gracelyn.

He screwed up his courage and started a conversation with her after services one day. Her parents were not keen on the idea of their daughter talking to a boy they knew nothing about, but John was always respectful and polite, and he was able to sway them with his easy manner and his evident devotion to his faith. Gracelyn liked him. After some time, her parents allowed him to come calling, and they would sit on the screen porch at the front of her house to talk.

One warm evening in the spring of 1987, John and Gracelyn sat on her porch swing when her parents went upstairs to retire for the night. By now, John was a familiar and trusted figure to them, so they just told their daughter to come inside by 10:00. After the parents went upstairs, they continued to talk for a while. Gracelyn moved closer to John, so close her thigh was touching his, and she took his hand. She placed it firmly on her thigh, then turned to John and said,

"Are you ever going to kiss me, country boy?"

John was startled by her boldness and he quickly stood up. Gracelyn took no discouragement in this, but rather got up to stand between him and the steps leading to the street. She put her arms around his neck. In his head, he heard his father's voice calling to him from the grave,

Whores! Trollops! The lot of them!

John's swelling desire overcame his guilt and he returned her embrace and kissed her. They returned to

197

the porch swing and continued. John was aroused. Gracelyn unbuttoned her white cotton blouse and placed his hand on her breast, which was small and firm. Their kissing grew more passionate and John slipped his hand inside the cup of her bra to feel the hard nipple within. Gracelyn was reaching for his belt buckle when the night air was punctured by her mother's voice calling from the window above.

"Gracie, say goodnight to that boy and come inside. It's almost 10:15."

Gracelyn giggled as she buttoned her blouse and called to her mother,

"Right away, Mom!"

She whispered to John, "Friday night. They go bowling on Friday night and they don't come home until after 11. Meet me at 9:00 in the woods behind the K-Mart on 17th. I'll bring a blanket!"

She kissed him one more time, then turned to go inside.

Friday night came. At 8:00 PM, Gracelyn's parents left with their bowling balls and told her not to wait up for them. At 8:40, she left her house with the hood of a sweatshirt pulled over her head and a blanket stuffed into her handbag. She waited at the edge of the woods for John Miller. At 10:30 PM, she dejectedly walked home, the blanket still in her handbag, and cried herself to sleep.

Sunday morning came, but John was nowhere to be

found among the congregation at church. Monday after school, she went to the rooming house where he lived. The owner told her John Miller had moved out last Thursday after paying up for the week. She never heard from him again.

John reached into the lower drawer of his desk and poured himself three fingers of Wild Turkey from the bottle he kept there, into the dirty glass he kept next to it. Weeping as he poured, he prayed, "Father, forgive me, for I am weak. Thy will be done, cleanse me of my sin with Thy holy fire!"

He tipped his glass to the portrait of Jesus and downed it in a single gulp. He followed it with another and took the bottle with him when he got up to leave.

10:30. Best be getting home.

Joshua lay on top of his comforter, unable to sleep, unable to escape his anguish. He could think only of Mary Elizabeth, and he repeatedly reached under his pillow to clutch the silver chain she had given him.

The clock on his bedside table read 11:45. He had heard his father come in a little more than half an hour ago, and he hoped to God he was in bed by now. He'd had to pee when he heard his heavy footsteps on the stairs, and he couldn't hold it any longer. Rising from his bed, he turned his doorknob silently and stepped out into the hall. He stopped dead in his tracks. His father stood just outside Anica's door, clad only in his boxer shorts. His back was turned to Joshua, who watched him for nearly a minute as he just stood there, breathing heavily. Joshua could not stifle his frightened gasp when his father put his hand on Anica's doorknob.

John Miller turned with an angry scowl on his face at the sound. He snapped at Joshua,

"Boy, what are you doing up? Go back to bed!"

"I - I have to, have to g-go to the bathroom," Joshua stammered.

"You're supposed to go before you go to bed!"

"I did, but..."

"But nothing, you little shit! Back in your room before I take my hand to you!"

John was nearly shouting now, which brought Agnes out of the master bedroom, and she quickly moved between her husband and her son.

"John! Your language! He just has to go to the bathroom!" In a much gentler voice, she told Joshua,

"Go on honey. Don't forget to wash your hands, and then get back to bed. It's very late."

Through the bathroom door, Joshua heard his mother's angry tone return.

"Why are you out here in your underwear? What are you doing outside Ani's door? Have you been drinking? Again? "

John Miller's tone changed markedly as he was confronted with his wife's fury. "I thought I heard a noise. I thought it was coming from in there."

"In your underwear? You have been drinking! What's that on your breath, bourbon? You swore to me you stopped."

Joshua flushed the toilet and washed his hands extra clean, grateful his mother had awakened to rescue him – and Ani. He had been terrified for her. When he emerged from the bathroom, he could still hear his parents arguing heatedly in their bedroom. Wanting no more of it, he retreated to his room. In time, the muffled shouts and curses subsided and he was finally able to sleep. When he awoke, he headed down to the kitchen for breakfast. His mother was talking to his sister.

"... so remember to lock the door to your room before you turn out the light. Promise me you'll do that, sweetie."

"Mom, you're scaring me," Anica pleaded.

Agnes Miller smiled and she took a less urgent tone, lying to her daughter,

"Well, we just can't be too careful! The paper said there have been some burglaries, more than usual, and the police want everyone to lock all of their doors until they catch them." She added, "It's just a good idea anyway, so promise." Raising her head to Joshua, she continued, "You, too, Josh. Promise me."

"I promise, Mom," Anica and Joshua said, almost in unison.

Like his mother, Joshua did not want Anica to be afraid, but he could not unsee what he saw. Thank God she had slept through the commotion last night. A pang of shame came over him when he thought of the night he had crept into her room, had stolen what she never knew had been taken. *Innocent. Vulnerable.* What was his father going to do in there? Joshua had never trusted his father. He'd thought he loved him once, but now he felt only anger and fear.

When Joshua got home from school that day, he took his baseball bat from the garage and put it under his bed. Once again, he was unable to sleep, tossing and turning until he heard his father come home. He waited for the sound of his feet on the stairs, but it didn't come. Half an hour passed, and his father remained downstairs. Having slept so badly the night before, he was too exhausted to keep his eyes open, and he fell asleep, his hand still on the hilt of his bat.

When he went downstairs in the morning, the sofa was half-covered in an old comforter. The throw pillows had been cast aside and a pillow from his parents' bedroom lay in their place. Puzzled and anxious, he asked his mother about it when he sat down to breakfast.

"Your father has been working late," she told him. "We thought it would be better if he slept on the sofa so he doesn't wake you kids up when he comes home."

Mom wasn't very good at lying. Dad had been

working late for years, but this was new and it came too closely after the events of two nights ago to be a coincidence. Still, Anica seemed to buy her story, so Joshua decided he should go along. In the days that ensued, he told neither his mother nor his sister that on each night since the incident in the hallway, he slept next to his bat, and he quietly crept into the hallway after Mom went to bed to test the lock on Anica's door. He'd known she wouldn't forget, but he still needed the peace of mind before he could sleep.

Anica

Anica wiped the mist from the bathroom mirror with her towel. She regarded her reflection this way and that. She was still thin and lean, but her form was softer, less angular, and her chest had started to pop. Regarding herself in profile, she still thought she was too flat, but she liked wearing the little bras her mother had bought her. They mostly flattened her out when she dressed, but without them, she was self-conscious about the telltale little bumps her breasts – at last, breasts! made in her clothes, especially in her leotards.

She understood what was happening to her body. Mom said it was how girls grew into women. She told her about how boys grew into men. Mom told her about a lot of things, all of it that she could, for which she was grateful since her father would let her have nothing to do with sex education in school.

Her father! She grew more frightened of him every day. She didn't like the way he looked at her, when he was home, which was rarely these days. There were no more Friday nights at the dinner table. They had even stopped going to church together, which Anica did not miss.

There was a time when she so wanted him to see her, just to notice her. He never came to her meets. Her mother had browbeaten him into coming to her big winter recital, but before that, she could not remember a time when he'd actually heard her play. She always brought home excellent report cards, but while her mother had lavished praise on her, she could not recall his ever mentioning them. He paid far more attention to Joshua's grades, and to his behavior in general. It was not the kind of attention she wanted for herself, but it was attention nonetheless. He'd missed her tenth birthday party two weeks ago, just as he'd missed all the others. Mom said it was because of his work, but she wasn't even sure he knew when her birthday was.

It was only recently that he'd started to notice her at all. After the recital, she stood on stage with the other finalists, with her bright red ribbon and a bouquet of flowers. He was staring at her from the audience, but he was neither applauding nor smiling. Just staring, with a look something like disapproval, but there was something else in it. Something scary. That night in the motel, he had slept fully clothed on the bed farthest from the door, while her mother slept between her and her father in the other bed. He'd not spoken a word to her on the drive back, but she had caught him several times looking at her in the rearview mirror as she sat in the back seat with her schoolbooks. It was the same look she'd seen after the concert, a frown but with something scary in his eyes.

Her thoughts turned to her brother. A change had come over him recently, too, but it was a change she loved. He looked at her adoringly, the way he'd done when they were both small and had been nearly inseparable. He'd stopped slacking on his share of the afterschool chores. He held her coat for her in the morning as they prepared to leave for school. He listened to her practicing her piano before dinner instead of staying in his room. He came to her meets and cheered for her. When she won first place on the balance beam, he ran to meet her as she left the floor. He hugged her, picking her up and swinging her around, and told her how proud of her he was. He hadn't been tardy to school for months, and there had been no phone calls from the vice principal.

Even more, since they'd returned home from Grandma Aggie's funeral, he suddenly seemed a lot more mature, more confident. He paid closer attention to his appearance, and had even asked Mom to take him to get his hair cut. She found herself feeling proud of her brother, something she hadn't felt in a long time. And she loved him. At her core, she had always loved him, loved him a lot, but she'd been so mad at him, so hurt by the things he sometimes said to her, that she hadn't let herself feel it for a long time.

Yet she worried for him. A few days back, she came straight home from school when her piano teacher took ill and canceled her lesson. She heard sobbing from upstairs. The door to Joshua's room was open. He sat at his desk with a half-finished worksheet lying on the floor beside his chair. In his hand, he held a fine silver chain with a small cross, the kind she saw in Grandma's house, with a tiny figurine of Jesus. It was the one Mary Elizabeth had given him when they'd said goodbye. He hadn't been without it since.

Tears streamed down his face. Anica was so moved that she wanted to cry herself – but right now, her brother needed her, and she quickly went to him, gently laying her hand on his shoulder.

"Mary Elizabeth?" She inquired, very softly, very gently.

Joshua nodded, trying to wipe his tears away with his hands. Anica got the box of Kleenex from his nightstand and brought it to him.

"Ani, it's so hard," he sobbed. "I miss her so much."

"Can't you write to her? Mom has her mother's address."

Joshua blew his nose and tried to stop the tears, but he couldn't.

"I did," he told her. He reached into his drawer and pulled out a pastel green envelope with a fancy border of wildflowers. It had been opened carefully so as not to tear the pretty paper. It was addressed to him in beautiful cursive, with a postmark from Cliffordsborough. Joshua handed it to her wordlessly and returned to dabbing at his eyes. Inside, on matching stationery, in the same beautiful cursive as the envelope, Anica read:

207

My Dearest Joshua,

I received your letter yesterday. I read it over and over. You say such sweet, wonderful things, things no one has ever said to me before. You wrote to me of how you love me, of how badly you miss me, and before I go on, let me swear that I feel these same things for you. Nothing has seemed right since you left. I think I've cried every night, and I'm crying now.

But this is why we cannot write to one another. It just makes me want to see you all the more, and this is a thing that just cannot be. You told me your family never travels. It is the same with mine. My father's business doesn't let him get away, and my mother is not well. She needs a new kidney and every few days she has to be hooked up to a machine to cleanse her blood. I could not leave her for anything right now, even for you.

And we are so young, dearest Joshua. We are not free to see each other, not in the way we want to, even if we did not live so far apart. It's so unfair! So unfair! But there is nothing we can do about it. I've told myself I can wait, wait forever if I must - but how could I ask the same of you? I know you are telling yourself the same thing, but I think we are kidding

209

ourselves. We are both going to change. I saw my brothers go through this, and as much as we might not want it, this will happen to us, too. You might meet someone, or I might, even if all I can think about now is you.

It hurts. It hurts for both of us. This cannot go on. Even if I could bear it, I would not wish this for you – I love you too much to be at the center of so much pain. But even though it hurts so much, the thought of how my life would be if we had never been together is even more unbearable.

I did not tell you this before, because I thought you would be uncomfortable. The real reason I came to you was because I was so happy when Mom told me you would be coming.

You were so nice to me at the reunion. You sat with me on the lawn and we ate cookies, and you got up to get me lemonade when I said I was thirsty. You paid so much attention to me, and you made me so happy. I was just a little fat girl that scared the other kids because her family owned the biggest funeral home in town. You made me feel special. When you went home, I asked my mom over and over again when you were coming back. She just kept telling me someday, someday. In time, I stopped asking her, but I never forgot you.

I grew out of my weight. Well, most of it, and you grew up so handsome. You really are a cute boy, even if you don't think so! And then you came to town. I waited for the right moment to go to you, and then I just said something so stupid! But the way you looked at me, the look in your eyes – I wanted to get you all to myself, and that happened, and it was wonderful. I think that for as long as I live, no one will ever make me feel the way you did that night.

Last summer, I did something foolish with a boy I thought I loved, but that was wrong. It was wrong thinking that I loved him when I was really just so flattered that a popular boy like him would take an interest in me. When that turned out to be a lie, I was hurt and mad, but he wasn't hard to get over.

You, Joshua, you are really my first. My first love, no one else will ever get to be that, and know this, dearest Joshua - I will always love you. Always. I think that always is an even longer time than never, and I hope that maybe someday we might see one another again and maybe we will be able to once again have something special.

But until that day, dearest Joshua, until

then we must be content with our memories of each other. I can't say goodbye, but we must get some living done, both of us, before we can meet again.

All of my love, dearest Joshua. All of my love.

Mary Elizabeth

Anica placed the letter carefully back into its envelope and set it down in front of Joshua. Now she was crying without shame. She bent to hug Joshua around his neck. He turned to her, slipping from the chair, falling to his knees, and held her tightly. He could not let her go, not only because he had never loved her more, but because at this moment, there was no one else in the world who could care for him so much as to share so much pain. His sister. His beloved, only sister. She would be someone else's sweetheart someday, but no one could ever take that away from him.

When they let go and dried each other's tears, Joshua opened the bottom drawer of his desk. There, underneath the Bible he never read, he kept his treasure box. It was a small, ornate wooden box with brass hinges that his grandfather had given his mother to keep for her firstborn before he died. It was lined on the inside with black velvet. His grandfather had placed four silver dollars inside, that had been minted in the late 1800s. Joshua had added some treasures of his own, including a small, smooth stone, one like countless others used for landscaping around the neighborhood, but this one was special. Anica had found it, after examining and discarding a hundred others, when she was not quite four years old. She'd clumsily wrapped it in brightly colored paper and had given it to him on his sixth birthday.

Joshua placed Mary Elizabeth's letter inside, and on top of it, the silver chain he had carried with him and had kept under his pillow since the day he last saw her. He returned the box to his drawer, placed his Bible back on top of it, and picked up his math homework from the floor. He asked Anica,

"Mrs. Simmons was out today. Do you know anything about this stuff?"

"No," she said brightly. "But I'll stay here with you and we'll try to figure it out."

John

John Miller did not look back as his bus left the city. Memphis had been good to him, but it was time for him to move on.

In the seat next to him was a duffel containing his clothes and his few possessions. In a front pocket of his trousers, he had seven hundred and fifty-nine dollars he had scrupulously saved from his earnings. The ride back to the county where he was born would take just a few hours, but John Miller was not going home. When he left the bus station, he went to the courthouse and obtained a certified copy of his birth certificate. He was 18 now, free to do what he chose. This being done, he walked back to the bus station to purchase a ticket to Chicago.

In his duffel, tucked into the pages of his Bible so it would not crumple, was a letter his boss in Memphis had given him. It was typewritten on company letterhead.

```
       To Whom it May Concern,

       This is to introduce John
   Miller, as fine a young man as I
   have ever hired. John has been one
   of my best workers, and it saddens
   me greatly that he has chosen to
   leave my employ. John is extremely
   punctual, he hasn't missed one day
   of work, and he works very hard.
       You only have to show him how to
   do something once, and he will
   soon show you how to do it better.
   Every man on my crew likes him and
   respects him even though he is the
   youngest man here.
       I will miss John, but I will
   tell you this: If you hire this
   young man, he will quickly prove
   his worth, and you will not regret
   it.

       Sincerely,

       Joseph A. Price, Proprietor,
       Price Construction Company
       Memphis, Tennessee
```

When John arrived at the bus station in Chicago, he
bought a newspaper and sat down on one of the
benches, circling want ads with a red ball point pen.

He found a furnished apartment that he could rent by the week, so long as he paid in advance. He found only a few construction companies that were hiring, which was a disappointment. He also circled an ad that read,

Help Wanted
Able bodied man to do odd jobs for small insurance agency. Duties to include cleaning, maintenance, stocking, and running errands. Experience preferred but not necessary. Apply directly to:

Vincent P. Cochran, Proprietor,
Cochran Insurance Agency
712 W. Woodbury St.
Chicago, IL

John took the small basement apartment he'd found in the newspaper. There were only two rooms and a small bathroom with a chipped cast iron tub. He had a small refrigerator, a sink, and a hot plate with two burners. There were an adequate number of mismatched dishes and glasses, a drawer with utensils, and some pots and pans. There was no telephone, but the owner of the house upstairs allowed him phone privileges between 6 and 8 PM in the evenings. It would be the nicest place John had ever lived.

His money would run out in a matter of weeks, so he needed to find work soon. He sent neatly handwritten letters to each of the employers he'd found in the paper. Only one of the construction companies he contacted got back to him, but they needed a journeyman carpenter with his own tools. John was discouraged, but he bought a newspaper every day and continued to circle ads.

A few days later, his landlady brought him a letter addressed to him from the Cochran Insurance Agency. John anxiously tore it open and he was elated that the man to whom he had written wanted him to come in for an interview. At 6 PM sharp, he called the number Mr. Cochran had given him. A man promptly answered, identifying himself as Vince Cochran. He was eager to talk to John and asked if he could come in the next day. John's landlady overheard much of the conversation and asked him if she could help him prepare for the interview.

John had a wrinkled suit with a white shirt and tie that he had bought in Memphis. His landlady – who wanted to keep him as a tenant – pressed his clothes for him. The next morning, John walked the 20 blocks to 712 W. Woodbury St.

Vince Cochran was a portly man in his mid-fifties, with thinning brown hair. He leaned heavily on a battered wooden cane when he walked. He invited John to sit down in a drably painted office with only

217

four desks. John handed him the letter of recommendation from his boss in Memphis, and Cochran put on a pair of small wire-framed glasses to read it. John saw him smile and nod.

"Mr. Price certainly seems impressed with you. I hope you don't mind if I call him."

John confidently assented, knowing that Cochran would call him anyway. Cochran picked up the phone and called Price Construction. After a bit of waiting, he said,

"Mr. Price, I have a young man here named John Miller. I understand..."

He said no more as he listened to the voice on the phone, smiling and nodding as he had when he read the letter John had given him. He smiled broadly when he hung up the phone.

The other desks in the office were unoccupied, but there were clear signs that people were using them. There were filing cabinets, typewriters, and some machines John didn't recognize. There was a wall with a lot of oddly-titled books about insurance, law, accounting, and sales practices. There were more books full of rates and regulations from several states. John understood little of it, but in a small rack on Vince Cochran's desk was one book he immediately recognized: a King James Bible. To go with it, a large portrait of Jesus hung on the wall over Cochran's desk. A number of papers in a basket on the desk were on

218

letterhead that said

**Christian Guaranty Life Insurance Company
To The Glory of God**

Cochran observed John's expressions as he
surveyed the portrait and the items on his desk.

"I take it you're a man of faith, Mr. Miller. Now, I
know I'm not supposed to ask you that and all, but I
know a God-fearing man when I meet one."

Cochran touched the hilt of his cane, which he kept
in an umbrella stand next to his desk.

"Mr. Miller, I don't get around too well, and I'm
here by myself all morning. I need a man who can do
things for me. This and that, things I can't do myself
any more. Then there's the sweeping, keeping things
put away where they belong, washing the windows,
and a lot of other things I can't think of right now."

"I did a lot of chores like that when I was younger,"
John said, keeping the bitterness out of his voice. "I
can do all those things, pretty much anything you
need."

John and Vince Cochran talked for nearly two
hours. They talked as much about faith and the
Scriptures as they did about the particulars of the job.
Cochran explained that the other desks were empty
because his people – two agents and a secretary –
started work in the afternoon and worked well into the

evening, when their clients and prospective clients were home. Cochran himself came in at 8:00 AM to handle business with the home office and the legal work, and he usually stayed into the evenings to join his agents in servicing and bringing in clients.

At the end of the interview, Cochran offered him the job. He told him it paid eleven dollars an hour – more than twice what he had been paid in Memphis. John eagerly accepted and told him he could start that very day.

Vince Cochran was impressed with John's thoroughness and his dedication. It was also evident to him that he was keenly intelligent, and that people liked him when they met him. One day, three years after John had started there, he asked him to sit down and talk. He told John he would like to take him on as an agent, but that he would have to do a lot of studying and pass a lot of exams in order to qualify. John was extremely flattered, but he was forced to admit he hadn't completed high school. Cochran waved it off and told him he could study for something called a G.E.D. concurrently with his other studies, and that he would have no trouble getting it.

John studied far into the night and every Saturday. In two years, he had an insurance license and became a full agent of the Christian Guaranty Life Insurance Company. He would no longer be paid by the hour, but would earn commissions on every policy he could sell. Cochran took a portion of his commissions to maintain his agency business, but John got to keep most of it.

He drummed up business by attending services and meetings at Evangelical churches throughout the area. Often speaking before groups, he had inherited some of his father's oratory talents, and in time became one of the company's best-producing agents. One day, Vince Cochran asked John to sit down with him. He had something important to discuss.

Cochran suffered from arthritis. It was not getting any better, he explained, and he was not getting any younger. The biting Chicago winters were hard on him, and soon, he would no longer be able to work the hours needed to run his agency. He had decided to retire to Arizona where the air was warm and dry. John wasn't sure what he was getting at. Was he losing his job?

"John, I need a good man to take over this agency. That man is you, and I'm not asking. You've nearly doubled the commissions we're bringing in, and thanks to that, I can retire."

Cochran produced a contract for John to sign. It stipulated that John Miller was to become the sole proprietor of the agency, on the condition that Cochran was to receive a percentage of the profits for as long as he had left to live. John smiled at his friend, took a nice fountain pen from the pocket of his crisp, white shirt, and signed it. The agents gave Cochran a party in the banquet room of a nearby restaurant, and John soon stood in the hall of the office building his – his! – agency occupied, watching as a workman scraped the lettering off the door and replaced it, in shining gold leaf, with the words

MILLER INSURANCE AGENCY

John worked tirelessly to build up his business. He started work at 7:30 AM each day, and he was usually the last one to leave. He had moved to a larger apartment not long after he started work for Vince Cochran, in a building only three blocks from the office. He remained there long after he started earning enough money to afford something more luxurious. He bought good suits for doing business, but otherwise, he had no need of luxuries. He read both of the major newspapers to keep up with events, but he used a computer only at the office and he did not own a TV.

He bought a rack of weights and he took vigorous walks to keep himself strong. He continued to study at home, far beyond what he needed to do to keep his insurance license current. He studied accounting, law, history, college level mathematics, and theology. There was not a minute of his waking day that he was not busy with something.

It was not enough. John was lonely. It wasn't

something that he thought about; it was something that pursued him in his few idle moments, and especially at night when he was done with his day's labors and preparing for sleep. The more he tried to evade it, the more it gnawed at him.

Chicago was a city rich in night life. Every neighborhood had attractions. He began to eat in restaurants, just to be around people other than his clients. There was a small cafe on his walk home from the office. The food was good there, and the people were friendly.

A server named Marcine was nice to him, and he liked her. She wasn't especially pretty, nor was she unattractive. She was just friendly, and John grew comfortable talking with her. He always tipped her a bit more than was customary. One evening, she returned with his credit card receipt. On the bottom, she had written a note that said, simply,

My shift is over at 9:00.

John looked up from his table, but Marcine was already with another customer, so he left for home.

At 8:40, John put down the trade magazine he was reading and looked at the note again. He glanced to the hallway that led to his empty bedroom and got up to get his coat. A familiar and unwelcome voice sounded in his head.

"Goin' out whorin', are ye Johnny?"
"Shut up, Pappy! I'm going to see a friend."
"At the gates of Perdition, you are."
"Y'all're dead, Pappy."
"Jest bidin' my time until the Resurrection.
Somebody gotta keep an eye on ye."
"I buried you once, Pappy. I can bury you again."

John buttoned his shirt and straightened his tie. His father wouldn't shut up, but he mostly ignored him now. Mostly.

John stood outside the doors of the cafe at 9:00. He observed Marcine through the windows as she filled out her time sheet and got her coat. He smiled at her as she walked through the front doors.

"Tall, dark, and handsome, and right on time!" she said, smiling back. John offered his arm and she took it. "There's a decent bar over on Ashcroft. Not much atmosphere, but it's quiet enough."

"I don't drink on weeknights," he told her, "but I'd enjoy the company." It was not a lie. John had tried to drink beer with his friends at Price construction when he was still sixteen, and it made him sick. He had not touched alcohol since.

There were few patrons when they entered, just a few locals watching a Bulls game. They took a table in the corner. Marcine ordered a glass of white wine, and John ordered a club soda.

"Just so you'll know," Marcine said, "I don't pick

224

up guys, really, I don't. I know I'm not much to look at, but you're such a nice fella."

"Don't sell yourself short, Marcine. And who's to say that's all a man can be interested in?"

"And charming, too! You're a true Southern gentleman, John. My mother's from Georgia. She's always telling me the men are better where she came from."

"Y'all gonna bother takin' her home, Johnny, or are ye just gonna do it out in the alley?"

"How long is it gonna take fer your corpse to rot, anyway, Pappy? Cain't be much left 'o that pine box we planted you in by now."

"Tennessee. Honestly, Marcine, I don't think it's much of a place to be from. It's like time forgot most of them. This German guy, Gutenberg. If it weren't for him, I'd never have gotten out of that place. Needle on the compass points this way, you know."

"Well, I can still tell you that most of the men around here aren't much to talk to. How come some girl hasn't snatched you up by now?"

"I run a business. Takes most of my time. But I reckon it doesn't have to take all of it."

"I grew up right here. My folks move to the suburbs, but I'm still a city girl. The waitressing thing is just temporary. The tips are good, and it lets me take classes during the day. I want to be a teacher."

"That's the other reason I got out of Tennessee.

225

Town only had one school, but they taught me there was something outside of there."

"Filled yer head with notions, they did. Further ye get from God's country, the closer ye get to Perdition, and looks to me like yer smack dab in the middle of it right about now."

"Don't interrupt me when I'm talkin' to the lady, Pappy. In fact, don't interrupt me at all."

"Heh heh. 'Lady.' Jest another word fer 'whore.'"

"I just wish I started sooner. I got married too young, and boy, was that ever a mistake. I'm divorced now. Thank God I didn't have children with him. Don't get me wrong, I love children, but it wouldn't have been right with him. I hope you don't mind."

"I done tole ye so. Gotta wonder how many other men she slep' with. Heck, boy, ye better look in the closet 'afore ye get yer pants off. Might be two or three of 'em waitin' in there."

"Ah, I made enough mistakes when I was young. Good thing you realized it when you could still get out. I kinda wish my momma would've gotten out and taken me with her. She didn't have much education, wouldn't've been much for her to start over with. At least my Pappy did us the courtesy of dying before it was too late for me."

"Now that's on you, Johnny boy. If ye ain't a been cavortin' with Satan's whores, then I wouldn'a got so mad at ye, an' my ticker mighta held up."

"Thought that mighta got to ye, Pappy."

Marcine frowned. "I'm sorry. It sounds like you and your father weren't close."

"We were too close. Just not in a good way. But that's enough about him. The dead need to rest."

"You gettin' this, Pappy?"

John and Marcine made small talk for an hour or so. It was getting late for a weeknight, so they decided to go.

"Can you walk me home, John? It's not good for a girl to be out alone at this hour."

"Here it comes, Johnny boy!"

"I would be most honored, Marcine." John offered his arm again, and she took it. Her apartment was four blocks from the tavern. John offered to walk her up the stairs.

"I would invite you in for a drink, but I remember what you told me earlier. It's late, you must be tired."

"Whaddya think it'll cost ye, Johnny? Y'all don't think yer gonna git it fer free, now do ye?"

"You know, it's not that late. I guess I can stay long enough for one drink. Do you have something non-alcoholic?"

John followed Marcine into her small apartment. It was sparsely furnished, but it was tidy. He sat on her sofa while she went to the kitchen for drinks. She emerged with a glass of wine for herself and a club soda for John.

"I hope you don't think this is too forward of me, John. It's just that a girl gets lonely."

John moved closer to her on the sofa. He bent forward to kiss her, and she let him, putting a hand on the back of his head. He put an arm around her and began kissing her more passionately.

"You feel that heat, Johnny? Them's the fires o' hell."

"I really don't do this. I really don't." Marcine said.

"Whores! Liars, ever' one o' 'em."

Marcine stood up and took John by the hand, leading him to the bedroom. She quickly removed her server's uniform, her slip, and her bra. Clad only in her panties now, she loosened John's tie and began unbuttoning his shirt. She followed by undoing his belt, and John took it from there. When he was down to his boxer shorts, Marcine laid down on the bed and John followed.

He resumed kissing her, fondling her breasts. She removed her panties and put her hand inside the waistband of his boxers. John had never gone this far with a woman before. His heart was racing. He slipped out of his boxers as he beheld her nude body.

"There it is, Johnny boy! That there's the doorway to hell. Satan done got ye now! Go on, boy! What're ye waitin' fer?"

"Get out of my head!" John shrieked aloud, startling Marcine. He turned from her and sat on the

228

edge of the bed, hands over his ears, anguish in his
face.

"John?" Marcine said, frightened and worried.
"What's wrong?"

"Marcine, I'm sorry. I haven't been…"

"John, it's alright, really it is. It happens. You're
just tired." Marcine laid a hand gently on his back.

"I have to go," he said.

John got dressed while Marcine put on a bathrobe.
She turned to him and said, "John, I'm sorry. This was
my fault. I came on too strong. It's just that you're so
nice, and I've been so lonely."

John turned and touched her cheek. His face held
only sadness. Without a word, he let himself out.

*"Y'all see, Johnny boy? I'm still lookin' out fer
ye."*

John was in no hurry to get home. He did not want
to pass the tavern where he and Marcine had talked,
nor did he wish to pass the cafe where she worked. His
apartment building was about ten blocks south. He
went east for four blocks before turning in that
direction.

He passed three corner bars on his way. One of
them played loud music that spilled out onto the street.
Looking east toward the skyline of the city, he saw the
lights of the big Loop skyscrapers twinkling faintly in
the chilly air. Big city, so little space. Day or night,
everywhere there were people, smelling of sweat,

tobacco, alcohol, and despair. Everywhere there were faces, too many of them looking like they would rather be somewhere else. Everywhere there were cars parked, lining the residential streets, creating narrow passageways for the drivers of other cars looking haplessly for a place to park. Profligate opulence lived side by side with grinding poverty. Most of all, there was noise.

He reached his apartment building. He needed a key card to get through the front door and another key to get into his apartment. He lived on the fourth floor of his building, but he eschewed the elevator, preferring to run the stairs, two at a time, to get to his floor. The hallways were narrow. It was a well-maintained building, free of trash, graffiti, and decay.

Nevertheless, through the walls of his apartment, he could hear the sounds of his neighbors' TVs, their babies crying, their parties, their arguments, their footfalls in the apartment above his, their toilets flushing, their showers. He could hear the sounds of traffic in the street below, the police sirens, and the rumble of the El two blocks to the east. Although he had grown accustomed to the noise, he sometimes missed the dead quiet of Arlo at night.

John knew what he had to do. He did not sleep, but called a cab to take him to Midway Airport. He purchased a round-trip ticket to Nashville and reserved a car at the airport there. The redeye flight he'd booked touched down at 9:00 AM. By 11:00, he was standing before the grave of The Reverend John Miller.

The grave was well-tended, like the others, but the fresh flowers that lay at the headstone told John his mother still lived nearby. His grandparents' farm was outside of town on a different road from the one he'd used to get here. He did not plan on visiting.

John stared at his father's headstone, standing in one place for a long time.

The Reverend John Miller
1916 – 1985
Pastor, Arlo Pentecostal Church
1964 – 1985

It was chilly, but by now John had grown accustomed to the brutal winters up north, so he wore only a light overcoat. He heard the sound of the rectory's screen door, a sound he remembered too well. He half-expected to turn his head and see his father approaching with a scowl on his face, but instead he saw the visage of the uninspiring man who had replaced his father at the pulpit. He was older now, so old that he would soon join the Reverend John Miller in the back row of the graveyard.

"Come to pay your respects, did ye? Not many do

231

any more. Just his widow and a few of the townspeople who remember him." The preacher studied John's face for a moment. "Johnny? Johnny Miller? Praise be, you've come home! Last anybody heard, you was in Memphis, but that was well nigh fifteen years ago."

The preacher offered John his hand and he shook it. "Yes, it's been a long time. But no, I'm not home. I just got some unfinished business here."

"I never met your pappy," the preacher continued, "but I know him by reputation. As righteous a man as God's ever given this green Earth."

John half-smiled. "Ever'body says somethin' like that. Y'all can't believe ever'thin' ye hear."

The preacher frowned. "Got somethin' to show ye," the preacher said. John followed him a short distance to a pair of graves that shared the same headstone. It bore the names of his grandparents. His grandfather had died just two years after John left Arlo. His grandmother passed not two years later. John bowed his head, then the two men returned to his father's graveside.

"Your mama remarried, y'know. Old Jake Thompson, after his wife passed on, he took a likin' to her. Good thing, too, she couldn't run that farm o' hers by herself. But she still comes here ever' Sunday and leaves them flowers there on your pappy's headstone. Y'all gonna go see her?"

232

"Weren't plannin' on it. Don't think there's much for us to say to each other. Weren't much we had to say when I was livin' under that roof over there." John gestured to the rectory. Looking to the fields beyond, he observed that the old barn was gone, only a few charred and crumbling fragments of its foundation remaining.

"Burnt to the ground, it did," the preacher said. "Lightnin' done struck it. Whole town come out to see it. Weren't nothin' to do but watch it burn. Dangedes' thin' y'ever saw."

John laughed out loud. "I'm in the insurance business, Reverend. Y'all know what we call them things? Acts o' God, we call 'em." John turned his eyes toward the heavens. "Praise be the Name of The Lord," he said, still laughing.

The preacher frowned again. "I'll take my leave o' ye so's y'all can take care o' that business ye mentioned." As he turned to go, he quoted Scripture.

> *For if ye forgive men their trespasses, your heavenly Father will also forgive you. But if ye forgive not men their trespasses, neither will your Father forgive your trespasses.*

"Matthew 6:14 and 15," John answered.
When the preacher had returned to the rectory, John, speaking aloud, addressed his father's headstone.

"Ain't no forgivin' today, Pappy. That ain't why I'm here. Now, y'all listen. I'm a-gonna find me a good woman and I'm a-gonna git hitched. Ain't nothin' in the Scriptures says anythin' wrong with that. I'm a-gonna have me a passel o' kids, and they ain't never gonna know anythin' about ye, Pappy. An' when I'm gone, ain't nobody gonna know about this here place."

"Y'all heard them words. If ye ain't be forgivin', ain't no forgivin' fer ye. Y'all gonna burn in hell, ye are! 'Course, I already knowed that."

John smirked. *"If thy brother trespass against thee, rebuke him; and if he repent, forgive him.* Luke 17:3. Y'all got somethin' to repent there, Pappy? Y'all think the Almighty mighta been tellin' ye somethin' when he done burnt down that barn over yonder?"

John continued, anger yet mounting in him. "Y'all used to quote Scripture when ye took me to the woodpile over there, remember that? Remember? Y'all took His name in vain, ye did! If I'm a' gonna burn in hell, y'all'll be right there with me. It'll be a reg'lar family reunion, it will." John turned his head toward the graves of his grandparents. "It will, ye hear me? It will!"

John realized he had been shouting. He saw the preacher's eyes gazing at him from the door of the rectory. He walked towards the door where the preacher stood at the threshold.

"Forgive me, Reverend. I been disrespectful," John

said humbly. The preacher regarded him gravely.

"I jes' hope yer business here is finished, son."
Once again, the preacher offered his hand, and once
again, John shook it.

"Tell my mother I'm all right," John told him.

"I'll tell her y'all were here, Johnny" he said.
"Anythin' else ye want me to say?"

"No." John told him. He got into his rental car and
drove back to the airport in Nashville, where he caught
his return flight. When his taxi dropped him off back
in Chicago, he was very tired. He laid down in his bed,
still in his clothes, and slept straight through until
morning.

The city and its noises were with him when he
awoke. Just a few hours in the country air of
Tennessee had cleared his head of the slight,
omnipresent stench of garbage, vehicles, and
unwashed humanity that he'd gotten used to. The city.
He had prospered here, but it was high time he moved
on.

John lived frugally and ran his business efficiently.
He had ample funds to relocate to the suburbs, where
there would be far fewer people about, and far less
noise. He decided on the community of Glen Park, a
fast-growing suburb to the south and west of the city.
He could lease a modern office twice the size of the
one he maintained in the city for half the cost, and he
could purchase a condominium for himself.

He relocated his business to an expansive office park. He found a sublet apartment where he could live until he found a place of his own. There was a townhouse development being built by Davis-Adler Construction across the street from his offices. It looked ideal.

A sign on the entrance to the development directed him to call or inquire at the company's offices. John liked to see the faces of the people with whom he did business. Late on a Friday afternoon in July of 2003, he inquired in person. There he met a young, pretty woman named Agnes Adler, whose job it was to show the company's properties to realtors and prospective buyers. He liked her, and he asked her to have dinner with him that very night.

Agnes was clearly a good woman, not like the rest of them had been. She wasn't forward or hungry or desperate. She respected his beliefs, and she listened to him. After a courtship of six months, they married. On October 17th, 2006, Agnes gave birth to a son. They named him Joshua.

Joshua

Monday. The weather was sunny and cool when Joshua emerged from the south door. He zipped up his hoodie and put his hands in its pockets. He wanted to get home and start on his math before Anica came home from piano. He still looked forward to doing his homework with her, but he was getting better at it on his own. He would do the easy ones and leave the word problems for later, when his sister could help him think. But it was now more about spending time with her than getting the work done. It was so good to have her back.

Today was the first day after Spring break. Joshua was actually happy to be back at school. Last week, Mom was dropping him and Anica off at Grandma's house before work. Grandma and Aunt Alice fed them well – too well, Joshua thought, but there was not much to do there. He and Anica passed the time watching TV, playing cards, and going to the park down the street from Grandma's house.

The park brought up fond memories for both of them. When they were little, Joshua would push Anica on the swings there. She insisted that he do it again, and he happily assented. She asked him to push her higher and higher, something that she was afraid of when she was small. When Anica was about as high as he could push her, she let go, did a somersault in midair, and stuck the landing perfectly. Joshua was delighted.

"I have got to see that again!" he told her. She did do it again, but this time she followed it with a double handspring into a twist, and stuck the landing again. She threw her arms up in a V, and took a bow. She then demonstrated her entire new floor routine for him. Joshua applauded and cheered her every move. He was so proud of her he felt like he could burst.

Not so long ago, he had been so jealous of the time she devoted to developing her talents that he'd failed to see the opportunities they gave him to be in her life. He learned to appreciate and enjoy the classical music she played, and he loved to listen to her practice. He found the things she could do in gymnastics to be truly amazing. He went to her meets, and he often went along with her and their mother to watch her Saturday practices.

Joshua and his sister were now as close as they had ever been, perhaps closer. His failures at school and with his father had driven him to keep her away. This should never have happened, he realized; those years need not have been lost. Even as a seven-year-old, Ani knew enough to form her own judgments. He was never a loser in her eyes. He had much to make up for, and he meant to make up for every minute of it.

As he watched her performing her somersaults, handsprings, twists, and walkovers on the wood chips of the playground, his sense of wonder for her grew deeper. To think this impossibly beautiful, immensely talented girl was doing this just for him! Ani was his life's blessing. His renewed connection to her had given him a confidence and direction all his own, making everything else easier to bear, every challenge easier to face.

The time they spent together at Grandma's was great, but by the end of it, they were happy to say goodbye to their grandmother and their aunt. There was only so much doting they could take. They would miss the corner park, but there was still the playground at Lincolncrest to look forward to now that the days were longer and they could go out together after dinner.

Anica had told him he inspired her to try even harder at the things she did so well. She put more emotion into her music, just knowing he was there to listen to her. Seeing him in the stands at gymnastics practice and at her meets inspired her to try more difficult – and dazzling – moves. Joshua thought that even if he did not have a shred of talent of his own, his pride in her was somehow making the world a better place. It had made his own world a place he wanted to be, and it had given him pride in himself.

Anica was helping him with his homework every day despite her busy schedule. She could read better than he could, and she helped him with some of the

239

lengthier and more difficult material he was assigned. She was not really coaching him. Once in a while, he would ask her a question about wording or spelling, but most of the time, just having her there with him took away so many of the obstacles that fell between him and his studies. When he got frustrated with his work, she would rub his shoulders, or do something to make him laugh, like walk around his room on her hands. They took breaks together over PB&J sandwiches in the kitchen. She played her piano for him. She even had him sit beside her and taught him a little bit about music. When they were finished, he could return to his studies free of frustration and fatigue. He caught up with all of his back work, and finished every new assignment on time.

He wished he could bring her to school with him to help him with the struggle there. He found nevertheless that she was still helping, even though his mind still wandered and he still struggled to read what his teachers put up on the whiteboards. He had come to realize that these things were not happening because he was lazy or stupid. He could not remember a time when it hadn't been this way for him; it was just the way he was. Mrs. Simmons understood, and she helped him. Mrs. Weinberg, the school psychologist, had reached out to him. But mostly, the knowledge that Ani would be waiting for him at home got him through when he faltered. He could raise his hand without feeling stupid. He could shrug it off and start over when he made a mistake.

It did not go unnoticed. His teachers affected a different attitude towards him, started to treat him like a regular kid. Even old, prune-faced Mrs. Addison stopped giving him a hard time, and nodded approvingly when she strolled by and looked at his work.

The other kids started to treat him differently, too. He felt less like an outcast and more like a kid who belonged there. As hard as his father had made life for him, it turned out that he'd been right about that. Kids started talking to him instead of making fun of him. He started talking back. He was even beginning to make some friends. Yes, it was good to be back.

Joshua rounded the building to start his walk home. Looking up the street he usually took, he saw Jesse Duncan and a couple of other large boys, loitering on the corner a block up the street. He wasn't going to take the long way to avoid them today. Joshua had things to do, and he'd had enough of Jesse Duncan. As he approached, he kept his eyes straight ahead and his pace steady, keeping his hands in the pockets of his hoodie as he passed them.

"Hey, Miller!" Jesse taunted him, "Can I go out with your sister?"

Joshua stopped and turned to face him.

"You got a thing for fourth graders, Jesse?"

"I got a thing for her! She is soooo-weet!" The boys he was standing with chuckled. Joshua was nonchalant, facing the three boys calmly, hands still in his pockets.

"Well," he continued, "I asked her the last time, and she told me she was busy for the rest of her life." With that, he turned to continue his way homeward, keeping his eyes straight ahead and his pace steady. Jesse's friends were laughing out loud now, obviously amused by Joshua's comeback. Jesse grew angry.

"Miller! Hey, Miller! You don't walk away when I'm talking to you!"

Joshua stopped. After a pause, he turned to address Jesse, looking him in the eye.

"You know, Jesse, we've been doing this since the third grade. When is it you're going to do that thing you're supposed to do to me, anyway? That thing I'm supposed to be afraid of? I don't think you were ever clear on that, and you know what, I really don't care. My girlfriend just told me we can't see each other any more and I'm pretty bummed about it. Not much you could do to make me feel any worse."

Jesse scoffed. "What kind of girl would go out with a loser like you?"

"You wouldn't know her. She doesn't think much of jocks."

Joshua had not budged. He still kept his hands in his pockets, his eyes trained on Jesse's.

242

"Can you even count, moron? There's three of us. We can kick your ass."

"Probably. I couldn't take any one of you," Joshua remarked calmly. He took one of his hands out of his pockets and pointed his thumb over his shoulder.

"Yeah, you guys can beat the crap out of me. And then those people working in their yard over there call the cops, and then you're all kicked off whatever team you're on. Let's see, it's baseball season, right? Probably no football next year, either, because you'll get expelled. What's your dad going to have to say about that, Jesse?"

"C'mon," Jesse told his friends. "We've wasted enough time on this loser!" The three extra large boys turned to go. Joshua put his hand back in his pocket and turned his back on them, resuming his steady pace homeward. They would not see the ear to ear grin spread across his face.

Agnes

"Mrs. Miller, I am so delighted you came in to see me. I'm Judy Weinberg, the school psychologist. We spoke on the phone. Will Mr. Miller be joining us?"

"No," she said flatly. "Does he need to be here?"

"No. We only need the consent of one parent to begin work on Joshua's 504. Before we start, I want to congratulate you for the work you have been doing with Joshua. His attendance record has been perfect since Christmas break. He's been handing in his all of his homework, and his grades have improved across the board, especially his math grade. He started the semester in danger of failing, but he's brought his grade up to a solid C. He's been seeing his math teacher after school, but she says he's doing better on his own."

Agnes smiled. "I'm proud of Joshua, but it isn't me."

"Did you get him a tutor?"

"No, his sister has been working with him nearly every day, and he's been trying harder. They're very close, you see."

"Oh, how sweet! Is she in college?"

"No. She's in fourth grade at Lincolncrest Elementary."

Mrs. Weinberg's eyes widened, but she went on, "Well, Mrs. Miller, if he can keep it up, it makes

244

things easier for us. We do everything we can for children like Joshua, but in the end, it comes down to motivation. It seems like Joshua has found his."

"Yes," Agnes answered. "He's grown up so much, just over the last few months."

A tear of pride fell from the corner of her eye. She continued. "Now this, this 504 Plan, you called it? What does that do?"

"Well, first we have to identify the areas where Joshua needs help. With your consent, I'll give him a battery of tests and give some questionnaires to his teachers to fill out. If you can give me the name of his pediatrician, with your written consent, we can get another form from them. I'll also send one home with you, and one for your husband."

"I'll just need the one, thank you."

Mrs. Weinberg frowned for a moment, but she continued,

"Once we complete the assessment, we can identify the accommodations Joshua needs that will help him become a more successful student. When we've decided on these accommodations, we will call you in to review them. Once you've approved, we can begin."

"I can't wait to start!" Agnes said optimistically. "And you just need me, right? It's just that my husband has his own business, and he works a lot."

It wasn't exactly a lie, she told herself.

Joshua

The warm sun washed over Joshua's face as he left
by the south door. Two and a half weeks, he thought to
himself happily, until school would be out for the
summer. He had done it! He had beaten the sixth
grade! His backpack felt light, perhaps because nestled
into the front pocket of his math folder was a unit test
with a grade of B+ written in red ink at the top. B+ ! It
was the best grade he'd gotten in math all year – in
fact, it was the best he could remember. Mrs. Simmons
had stopped him briefly at the end of class and told
him this grade would bring his semester grade up to a
C+, and he would finish the year with a B – if he
handed in all his homework and got a B or better on
his next and final test.

He could not wait to see Anica when Mom brought
her home from gymnastics. She had worked with him
every day for weeks to help him get his homework
done, and he knew how proud of him she would feel
today. He didn't think anything could make him feel
happier.

He felt a light tug on his elbow. He stopped and
turned and there, standing not three feet from him,
resplendent in short shorts and a tank top that barely
met the dress code, was Becky. Becky Lindstrom!
Joshua involuntarily opened his mouth in an
astonished gasp.

"Oh, I'm so sorry Joshua! I didn't mean to startle you!" she said. If he could taste the sound of a girl's voice, hers would be like cinnamon and honey. He had not heard her speak since third grade, and she had never spoken directly to him before this at all. And she even knew his name! Could this actually be happening to him?

"It's me, Becky, Becky Lindstrom. We were in Mrs. Marcus's third grade class together. Do you remember me?"

Joshua remembered her. He'd remembered her every day since he first saw her.

"Y-yes, of course, Becky. You sat at the table behind me. Your homework was always on top when you passed it forward. I remember how pretty your handwriting was. And your paper always smelled like strawberries."

Becky smiled at him. Becky smiled at him! He felt as if his whole body had turned to water.

"Oh, I remember those, those silly scented pens my mom used to get me. There were some that smelled like coconut and others that smelled like watermelon, but I liked the strawberry ones. I can't believe you remembered that!"

"I remember a lot of things," Joshua told her. "You had a bright blue backpack with sparkles on it. And you had sparkly blue laces in your shoes. I liked the way they picked up the sunlight when you walked."

Joshua was in uncharted waters here. He couldn't believe he'd gotten so many words out of his mouth without stammering.

"Hey," Joshua continued, "doesn't your mom always pick you up at the north door?"

"Trying to get rid of me?" she said coyly.

"Oh, no, no, I, uh, uh..." Damn. There it was, the stammer.

"I'm teasing you, silly! No, I called my mom when class let out and told her it was such a beautiful day I'd like to walk home. I go this way for a few blocks. Can I walk with you?"

Joshua was really in uncharted waters now. On what ocean? On what planet even? But,

"Yes, Becky, I'd like that. Oh, wow! You still have the same sparkly blue laces in your shoes!" That felt stupid, Joshua thought.

"They're not the same ones, but yeah, I like them. Blue, it's my color I guess."

"I like it too," Joshua offered. Then, "I like how, your eyes, I like how the things you wear go with your eyes." Now he'd gone too far, he thought, but the words had just seemed right. For years on end, Joshua had been trying to think of something to say to her. He'd played out so many imaginary conversations in his head, but he never thought he could come up with the right thing to say to break the ice with her, something she wouldn't laugh at or take offensively.

The ice was broken now. She'd done it for him.

"What a sweet thing to say! Thank you!"

She looked and sounded sincere. Did she really like what he was saying to her? Then he remembered, trust. There could be no love without trust, and he'd loved her for so long. No, that wasn't quite right. He wanted to love her for so long, but he thought she outclassed him by so much she would never know or care that he existed. Yet here she was now, happily chatting beside him, the bright sunlight in her yellow hair, her shoelaces sparkling as she walked.

In this moment, his feelings for her changed from hopeless infatuation to something else. Something hopeful. Something good. Most of his perceptions about Joshua Miller had been wrong. It followed that whatever he believed others thought of him might also be wrong. He never knew what Becky thought about him, because he believed that she never thought of him at all. He was wrong about her, too. She caught up with him and tugged at his elbow, just because she wanted to talk to him. To Joshua Miller. It was too much to process in the moment, because the moment was far too pleasant for introspection.

All he was consciously thinking about was what to say next. He realized that it wasn't something he had to think about too hard. She had drawn him out so easily. It felt nice.

"What was it like, living in California?" Joshua

249

asked.

"You remembered that, too! Well, when we moved here, I really missed it, but my father, he's a lawyer. He was offered a partnership at a big law firm in the city, and it was just too good for him to pass up. My first winter here, I thought I was going to die!"

"That one was awful. Ani and I thought we would freeze to death walking home from school."

"Ani's your little sister, right? I think I remember seeing you together at Lincolncrest. She's adorable."

"You should see her now!" Joshua proclaimed proudly. "Yeah, Ani's really great. She a gymnast and she's really good. You should see all the medals and trophies she's got. I watch her meets. It's like she can fly or something! She gets up on this thing, the balance beam – it's like four inches wide, and she does back flips and stuff on it. I don't think I could even stand up on the thing."

Joshua was animated, talking with his hands, while Becky watched him, a small, amused, satisfied smile on her face. She had never seen Joshua smile so much. She'd hardly seen him smile at all, for all the years she'd seen him and thought of him. It made him so much cuter.

Joshua went on. "And her piano! She's amazing! She took second place in her age group in the whole freakin' state a couple of months back! She like, started taking lessons from this Russian lady when she was three. Only three, can you imagine that? She plays classical music. You know, I never knew I liked classical music, but now it's all I want to listen to. Isn't that funny? And you wouldn't believe how smart she is. She's only in the fourth grade, but she helps me with my homework, and my grades are better now. I don't know what I'd do without her."

She looked at him, so sincere again. "You love her a lot, don't you?" More seriously, "You're lucky. I wish I had a brother. Or a sister, somebody close like that. I don't even have a cat. My mother says she's allergic."

Loneliness. Joshua knew this. Another of his assumptions about Becky was wrong, but he'd made the same mistake before. Pretty girls can be lonely. And she thought enough of him to confide in him.

"I didn't know you were an only child," Joshua told her. "All of my relatives have big families. Mom wanted to have more kids, but after Ani, she wasn't able to."

"After me, they didn't want any more. Well, I think my father did, but my mother didn't. She probably didn't like what it did to her figure. Oh, what am I saying, I shouldn't be talking about her like that. But she does make a big deal out of being attractive. She was her homecoming queen in high school. Then there was the sorority, and then it was landing the guy at the top of his class at U.C.L.A Law School. I shouldn't

251

judge. It worked for her."

"I've seen your mom. You're prettier." *Oh, my God, Miller, did you really just say that?*

She smiled at him again.

"You meant that. You really are sweet. You know, a lot of boys, they look at me, but then they act so silly. You're not afraid to say what you feel. I like that.

"So anyway, about California," she continued. "It's warm and sunny there most of the time, but there are so many people! People, sitting in their cars, going nowhere. And nothing is really green unless they use tons and tons of water to keep it that way. But after that first awful winter, I was outside and I saw the green shoots coming up from the ground. Daffodils, then the tulips. Then the forsythias. I thought I hated the rain, but it makes everything so green, and the trees! I love it when the trees bloom. I never saw anything like that in L.A. Oh, how I love spring!"

Joshua realized that he'd never really known much about Becky Lindstrom, only that she was very pretty and that all the other boys thought so, too. And that she had nice handwriting that smelled like strawberries. Now she had a personality, and she had feelings he understood. He was still stunned by her beauty, but now, she was someone he could actually talk to. He was surprised at how much at ease he felt with her.

"But really," Becky said, "one place is as good as

any other. It's the people you're with who make a difference."

With that, Becky touched his forearm. Very lightly, and very briefly, but he knew what it meant when a girl did that. She liked him. He was likable, he knew that now. There was no cause for incredulity. This was real, and it was very, very nice.

Until now, Becky had avoided any loaded questions.

"Do you have a girlfriend?"

Joshua felt a sting in his heart. "No. I did, but she lives really far away, and it was just too hard for us to see each other."

"So now?"

"No. No one since. I'm too shy."

Becky smiled at him and lightly touched his forearm again, lingering there this time.

"Well, you're doing alright with me," she said cheerfully.

They had reached the intersection where Becky would turn to walk to her neighborhood. She paused to face Joshua. He had never stood this close to her before. Her eyes were the most beautiful shade of blue he had ever seen. She had a little birthmark on her neck. Her ears were pierced twice, close together, with four tiny topaz studs catching the sunlight. There was a small, faint scar on her left knee. Her legs were shapely and defined, like Ani's. Her breasts were small, and her stomach was flat. One of the straps of her bra had slipped out onto her shoulder, frilly and yet another shade of blue.

"Well, this is me," she told him. "Guess I'll see you in school tomorrow?"

"Yeah, yeah. In school."

She took a few steps away from him. Joshua paused to watch her as she walked. Her yellow hair hung in a ponytail, tied with a sparkle blue scrunchie. Her shorts fit her perfectly. He liked what he saw, but it would be rude of him to leer. As he turned to go home, Becky turned around and approached him again.

"Say – tomorrow is Friday. Me and some of my friends are going to the Dairy Queen on Sullivan Street after school. That's only a couple of blocks from you. Maybe I'll see you there?"

"Sure Becky, I'll see you there. That sounds nice."
Wow, she even knows where I live!

"Hope so," she said, turning to go again. His initial impression of her so long ago was that she was the prettiest girl in the world. He still thought so, but she was so much more than a pretty girl to look at now. It was another four blocks to his house. His feet did not touch the ground once.

His mood abruptly turned from elation to worry when he rounded the corner and saw Aunt Alice's car in the driveway of his house. She was standing on the front stoop, and Anica was beside her, tearful and afraid. She ran to him when she saw him hurrying up the block. Aunt Alice waddled slowly behind her.

"Josh, Josh," she sobbed. "It's Mom. She was at work and she started bleeding from..." Anica knew the word but could not say it "... between her legs. Bleeding bad. She had to go to the hospital in an ambulance. She's there now. She's having an emergency..."

"Hysterectomy." Aunt Alice completed it for her. "Come on, it's just us, we need to go there now. Your Uncle Alan is in Houston. He and Aaron won't be coming in until tomorrow."

They crawled into into the back seat of Aunt Alice's Toyota Corolla. Her seat was pushed back so far they both had to squeeze in behind the passenger seat – why would such a big woman own such a little car, Joshua had often thought. He held Anica close to him all the way to the hospital, and she buried her head in his chest, sobbing, the way she had done when she was little. He took her hand when they got out of the car and she held it tightly.

Aunt Alice told them to wait while she talked to a volunteer at the hospital entrance. She picked up the phone and said something Joshua couldn't hear. After a couple of minutes, she looked up at Aunt Alice and pointed to some elevators as she mumbled something more. Aunt Alice gestured urgently for the children to follow her. Anica peered into her brother's eyes in the elevator, as if pleading for him to tell her it was all going to be alright. He wished he could, but in truth he was as distraught as she. He was holding it together because at this moment, she needed him.

They followed Aunt Alice down a murky gray hallway until they came to the waiting area for surgery. She told the children to be seated while she talked to the nurse at the desk. The waiting room was crowded, but they found a long row of chairs with three empty seats, too far from the desk for them to hear anything. Anica buried her face in Joshua's chest again. Finally, Aunt Alice came over to join them. She could barely fit into the empty chair next to the children.

"She's still in surgery," Aunt Alice told them.

"W-will she be all, alright?" Joshua stammered.

Aunt Alice told them that a doctor would come out to talk to them in a few minutes. Dread began to overwhelm Joshua, but Anica – she was so afraid, holding him so tightly. Joshua clamped his jaw and bit back the tears that were trying to break free.

After an eternity – or had it been just a few minutes – the desk nurse called to Aunt Alice as a doctor clad in green surgical scrubs stood by, his face mask lowered around his neck. They hurried to the desk.

"Agnes –" He looked at the children and smiled. "They're closing now. Your mother lost a lot of blood, but we were able to stabilize her. It wasn't an easy surgery – she should have had this done a long time ago – but we think she's going to pull through it just fine."

Joshua's crushing anxiety turned to relief. Anica, however, was still tearful and upset, clutching Joshua's hand tightly. She looked up at the doctor and told him, pointedly,

"I want to see her! I want to see my mother!"

A tall man, the doctor dropped to one knee to face her eye to eye. His voice and manner grew gentle.

"Sweetheart – oh, you're so pretty! – Sweetheart, she will be coming out of the OR soon, but she'll be in recovery for some time, and the ICU after that. We're not supposed to allow children in there, but I'll see to it you and your brother can get to see her for a few minutes, okay?"

The doctor's kindly manner soothed her. In a much calmer voice, she asked him

"When?"

He glanced at a wall clock and told her,

"It's 5:00. I expect she'll be conscious and out of recovery in a few hours."

The doctor took a small pad of paper from the nurse's station and scrawled a note on it, which he gave to Aunt Alice.

"Room 410B," he told her. "8:30. You should get something to eat." To Joshua, he said,

"You keep on taking such good care of this pretty

lady, all right?" He turned from them and disappeared into an unmarked door nearby.

"What does the note say?" Joshua said.

Aunt Alice told them, "He's chief of surgery here. That says enough."

The food in the hospital cafeteria was varied and quite good. Joshua took a hamburger, French fries, and a wedge of pecan pie. Anica got a small plate with a piece of lemon chicken and a spoonful of mixed vegetables. Aunt Alice filled her tray with something smothered in brown gravy, a lot of side dishes, and two desserts. Joshua and Aunt Alice ate heartily while Anica picked at her food. Aunt Alice scolded her gently, "Ani, dear, you have to eat something. Your mother needs you to keep your strength up."

Anica did her best to finish her chicken and most of her vegetables. Over his pecan pie, Joshua said,

"Aunt Alice? I left my backpack in your car. I should get to my homework while we're waiting."

Aunt Alice deadpanned him and said, "Who are you? And what have you done with my nephew?"

The humor finally brought a smile to Anica's face. She asked Joshua, "How did you do on your test today?"

Joshua had forgotten all about how much he wanted Anica to see his good grade. Joshua beamed at her and said,

"Wait 'til you see!"

Joshua and Anica passed the time in the waiting room outside room 410B sitting close together on a sofa, while Joshua studied his lessons. Anica kept her arm around her brother and read along with him. At 8:30, a nurse came out to them and said they could see their mother now, but only for five minutes. She was awake but very weak.

Anica started to cry again when she saw her mother, pale and damp in a hospital gown, with IVs, tubes, and wires everywhere. Agnes motioned her to come closer with the one hand she had free and did her best to embrace her. She then took Joshua's hand, as Anica took his other. In a raspy voice, she spoke weakly,

"Joshua, watch over your sister." Then, "Alice, take them home with you for the night. Mother will be delighted to have them."

The nurse interrupted them, telling them they would have to leave now. Anica began to sob again. Joshua threw his arm around her and held her close as they left the horrible room.

They were to stay with Aunt Alice and Grandma tonight? For the first time since the crisis began, Joshua thought about his father. Mom had nearly died today and she was here now, covered in tubes and wires. Where was he? Why wasn't he with his wife?

Aunt Alice was reading his thoughts.

"I've been trying to get hold of your father all day.

No one is answering at his office and he's not answering his cell."

Joshua had no room to worry for his father. It had been weeks since he'd even seen him. He would leave the house early in the morning and return late at night, still sleeping on the sofa. Joshua always stayed up for a while after he heard his father come in, his baseball bat on his bed beside him. This continued into the weekends. Mom had told her children things had gotten very busy for him at work and he had to stay away so much to keep up. Even Anica knew she was lying at this point, but both of the children were more at ease when he wasn't around, so they let it go.

But now Joshua was mad at him. Mad as hell. He should be with his wife. He should remember he has children. He had always been stern and cold with them, but at least he had been there.

Grandma's house had only one spare bedroom, with two twin beds. They had not slept in them since they were little. They had no pajamas. Joshua could sleep in the jeans and polo shirt he'd worn to school, but Anica had worn a long skirt with a ruffled blouse that would be uncomfortable. Aunt Alice found her something to sleep in, one of her grandmother's dowdy nightshirts. She changed into it while Joshua waited respectfully outside of the room. It was short enough that she did not trip over the hem, but it was much too big on her. It made her look so small, Joshua thought.

Aunt Alice bade them goodnight and left the room, closing the door behind her. Grandma was already asleep. Anica was curled up in the other bed, but her eyes were wide open and she still looked so afraid. The day had been very stressful for Joshua and his own emotions were running riot. He got under his own blankets and turned off the table lamp on the nightstand they shared.

"Goodnight, Ani," he said, softly.

"Goodnight, Josh," she said, her voice unsteady. She is still scared, he thought. He hoped she could get some sleep. He hoped the same for himself. Right now, it was useless. He knew he was tired, but he kept turning over the events of the day in his head. It had started out so well. Mom had seemed fine when he and Anica went off to school. Then came third period and his triumph on his math test. The entire school had been in a happier mood with the beautiful weather. And there was that incredible walk with Becky.

Becky. How she had looked today, in those short, tight shorts and that thin pastel blue top. Those eyes. The sound of her voice. The smile that turned him to water. The sparkly shoelaces like the ones he'd liked when they were younger. Joshua could feel some of the tension draining from him. Perhaps he would be able to sleep after all.

"Josh?" a little voice from Anica's bed brought him out of his reverie. "Are you still awake?"

261

"I'm here, Ani."

"Josh?"

"Ani?"

"Josh ... can you ... can you hold me until I fall asleep?"

Joshua remembered how Anica had pleaded with Mom to stay with her when she was little. She'd been afraid of the dark, and Mom couldn't leave unless she left the door to her room open and the bathroom light on. When Anica was especially troubled, their mother would relent and curl up next her, holding her lightly until she fell asleep. She had long ago outgrown her fear of the dark, but right now, this was the same scared little girl he remembered.

Joshua crossed to her bed. He laid down quietly, on top of the blankets, and Anica moved in close to him. He put his head on her pillow and his arm around her. Anica, in turn, wrapped her arm around his, pulling his hand into her shoulder. His clothing and two heavy blankets were between him, but he could still feel the tension that gripped her. Her long, silky brown hair spread on the pillow next to his cheek. Joshua held his sister as though he was using his body to shelter her from the cold. Soon, he could feel the tension draining out of her. Her breathing was becoming slower and more regular.

Ani, so beautiful, so close now, close by him in the dark. Joshua thought back to the night he had crept into her room. His conscience had stopped him from touching her, and he'd felt so ashamed afterwards. He could never share this with her, he thought. He kept few secrets from her now that they had become so close again. The shame he still felt from that night would haunt him for a long time, maybe forever. If anything good had come of it, it made him understand that anything he did, any time he lied, any time he took something he didn't deserve to have, there was no such thing as getting away with it.

Anica had nestled into him, wrapping him around herself like a blanket. Joshua began to move away, his shame sinking him into despair. Yet when he moved, Anica pressed his hand more tightly against her shoulder, and she moved with him, keeping her body close to his. She trusted him completely now. Whether or not he was deserving of that trust, she needed him. He pushed his shame back down inside himself and lightly gripped Anica's shoulder. She squeezed his hand in return.

A few moments later, her hand relaxed and her arm slipped down onto the mattress. She had fallen asleep. Joshua gently removed his arm and slid off of her bed to return to his own. He found that as he had comforted his sister, she had comforted him as well. When he came to his senses during that shameful act months ago, it ultimately put an end to years of sniping and bickering, years of taunts and insults, years that

263

needn't have been, if he'd only known what he knew now: *love forgives*. When Joshua believed himself to be in love with her, he treated her with love. In a very short time, she began to return that love, love she had never lost, but had been keeping for him. She had forgiven him. Perhaps one day he would confess to her. Perhaps she would forgive him even that.

Daylight poured through the thin curtains of the bedroom windows. Joshua rubbed sleep from his eyes and looked outside. The sun was already high above the horizon. The clock on the nightstand read 10:09. He was missing school! As he got his wits about him, remembering the drama of yesterday, he realized that was not important right now. He looked over at Anica's bed. She lay on her side, her face turned toward his, eyes closed despite the brightness of the room. Joshua crossed to her bed and knelt beside her. He brushed a hair away from her face and kissed her, very gently, on the cheek.

"I love you, Ani," he whispered.

Anica opened her eyes and lifted a delicate hand to touch his face.

"I love you too, Josh."

A knock came softly on their door.

"Come in," Joshua and his sister said in unison.

Aunt Alice entered the room. Joshua observed that she barely fit through the door.

"Oh, good, you kids are up. I called your schools, I

264

told them what happened and that you wouldn't be in today. Grandma and I decided to let you sleep. You needed it."

"Mom?" Anica asked urgently.

"She's still in intensive care, but they think they'll be able to move her to a room tomorrow. Her nurses said she was awake and alert, and asking about you."

Joshua liked the sound of that, but his anger was rising in him again.

"Dad?"

"Still no word. I left several more messages on his voicemail, but nothing yet. You must be worried about him, too."

"I guess." And under his breath, "but not in the way that you think."

"Let's go downstairs and have breakfast with Grandma. Then we'll get over to your house to get you some fresh clothes. You might be staying here for a while."

That was all right with Joshua. He wanted to sleep in the same room with Anica, to watch over her as their mother had told him. The more he thought about his father, the more angry he became. He didn't want him coming near her again, and he would lay down his life to stop him.

Aunt Alice pulled into the Miller driveway a little after noon. Using her key, she opened the front door.

"John?" she called out. "John?" more loudly this

time. She entered the house and the children followed her. Joshua went to the kitchen and opened the door that led to the garage. It was empty. The sofa had not been disturbed since yesterday morning. He ran upstairs to check the master bedroom, but the bed had been made, in the way that his mother always made it. The sinks and towels in both of the bathrooms were dry.

"I don't think he's been here, Aunt Alice." Joshua called from upstairs.

On his way down, he passed his sister on the landing.

"Ugh, I really need a shower," she told him.

Aunt Alice glanced at her watch. "Josh, I have to run an errand for your grandmother. She needs a prescription from her doctor's office, and they close early on Fridays. It's not far. I should be back in half an hour. Do you think you can hold down the fort here while I'm gone?"

Joshua did not think so, but he was through with being a coward. He told her to go ahead, they'd be fine.

He watched from the window as Aunt Alice squeezed into her Toyota and disappeared down the street. He heard Anica start the shower in the bathroom upstairs. He was thirsty. He went to the kitchen for a glass of water and stopped cold at the entrance.

John Miller sat in his customary chair at the kitchen table. His clothes were disheveled and there was a nasty cut on his forehead that had barely scabbed over. His face was flushed and his eyes looked wild. On the table before him was an open bottle of Wild Turkey whiskey that was nearly empty. Near the table was an open door that led to the basement. The basement! Joshua had forgotten to look there, but no one ever went down there. It was half crawl space and contained nothing but some forgotten household junk and a bunch of spiders and other crawly things that Anica was terrified of.

"I thought that tub o' lard would never leave." he said.

"D-dad." Joshua stammered, "E-everybody is, is l-looking, looking for y-you."

"When y'all gonna learn to speak English, boy?" John barked at him. He spoke in a drawl far more pronounced than the mild Southern accent he always had. Joshua did not know the man he was now facing.

"Ah, I know all about yo' mama," John continued. "I think yer fat aunt damn near busted my phone with all them messages she left."

He reached for the bottle and took a long pull that drained it. He hurled the bottle past Joshua into a corner, where it shattered. He continued,

"Y'know, I'm s'prised that thing of hers didn't bust a long time ago, the way your sister done tore it up on her way into this world. S'prised that purty li'l gal didn't turn out to be a retard like you."

Joshua was terrified. With the sound of the shower still running upstairs, Joshua needed to change the subject away from his sister.

"W-what hap, happened to your, your car?"

His father now mocked him. "Wah What done hap happened to my my car is that I done run it into a light pole over on Sullivan Street. S'pect it's in the impound lot by now," he chuckled.

Sullivan Street. Becky. Friday. Joshua was surprised that popped into his head, but his mind was trying to evade the horror unfolding before him. He heard the shower shut off upstairs. Anica always took some time in the bathroom before she came out. It was unlikely she could hear them over the sound of the ventilating fan. *Ani, for God's sake, stay upstairs.* Joshua needed to keep his father talking.

"H-how did you, you get home? W-when?"

" 'S only a coupla blocks, dumbass. I reckon I been here since around four. Hard to find this place in the dark. 'Spose maybe I shouldn'a told you kids to turn all the lights off." He chuckled again.

"Passed out right here for a while," he said. Joshua looked at the floor to see a small patch of dried blood he had missed before. *How could I have been so stupid! Ani, Ani, please stay upstairs!*

"Got up a couple o' hours ago. Thought I oughta

check out the house some, since I ain't been home much. I thought I'd start with that pigsty you live in. Y'all hire a maid or somethin'? Hell, fer a minute, I thought I was in the wrong house. Found some interestin' things up there, though. What was y'all plannin' to do with this?" John reached under the table and pulled out Joshua's baseball bat. Before he could think of an answer, his father continued,

"And how long's it been since y'all looked inside o' this?" John produced Joshua's Bible.

"Y'know, right there I thought I might consult the holy scriptures fer some guidance in my time of trouble," he continued, "But then I found that dandy li'l box o' your'n. And what do y'all think I found when I looked inside?"

John reached into his shirt pocket and produced Mary Elizabeth's necklace. In spite of his terror, Joshua confronted his father angrily.

"That's mine! Mine! Give it back!"

John's face twisted into a mask of rage. "Your'n? This, this abomination, this idolater's cross? 'S like them damn fools don't even know He done rose from the dead! Where did you get it? Who give it to you? That ol' biddy done give birth to yo' mama?"

Joshua's rage rose to match his father's.

"The girl I love! The girl I love gave it to me! Now give it back!"

"A girl? A girl done give you this? One o' Satan's

269

whores done give you this?"

John stood up, dropping the necklace onto the table, and reached for his belt buckle. He wrapped the end of his belt around his hand and charged toward Joshua.

"Only thing I'm a-givin' you is a ass-whuppin'! I shoulda done this a long time ago!" Joshua could not make it to the door and he retreated into the corner with the broken bottle. He tried to fight his father, but he was too big, too strong. He grabbed the collar of Joshua's shirt and slammed him against the wall.

"Now git them pants down, boy. We do this with yer pants down!"

John let go of his collar and Joshua tried to make a break for the door. John caught him by the waistband of his jeans and yanked on them viciously. Off balance, Joshua tried to catch himself, but ended up whacking his forearm hard on the edge of the kitchen table. He fell hard on his shoulder and landed face down. Searing pain gripped him where he fell.

"I ain't gonna bother with them pants," John uttered. He began striking Joshua hard on his buttocks, very hard. The blows got harder and faster. Joshua tried to lift himself up with his uninjured arm, but his father stomped his foot on the back of his ribcage, slamming him viciously back onto the floor. Joshua felt something crack and another pain, deeper in his body, that radiated from inside of his ribcage outward, like being punched in the stomach, but worse.

270

Close to passing out, Joshua suddenly heard his sister's scream.

"Ani! No!" Joshua shouted.

"Daddy, Daddy stop! You're hurting him!" Anica shouted through tears.

John did stop, but it was to turn towards Anica, still in her bathrobe.

"I mean to hurt him!" he hurled at her. Lunging for her, but missing, he cried, "I got somethin' else in mind fer you, you little tramp!"

Free for a second, Joshua turned agonizingly onto his side. With his unbroken arm, he grasped the neck of the broken bottle from the corner where he lay. With all the force he could muster, he jabbed it hard into his father's calf, tearing through his trousers and biting deep into the flesh below. John's knees buckled and he howled in pain. Blood gushed from the wound.

"Ani! Run! Run!" Joshua shouted.

She hesitated a moment to look into Joshua's eyes. Seeing the desperation there, she did turn and run. John made to catch her, but he howled in pain again when he tried to take a step. He struggled to get his footing, then turned to Joshua and resumed the beating, this time on his arm and chest.

"Run, Ani! Don't stop!"

Fleeing to the living room, Anica tried to fight her panic. She should not leave her brother, was her first thought, but she knew she could do nothing to stop her

271

powerful father.

Jessica's! Of course! She ran to the front door to get help. When she opened it, help was there. Two uniformed policemen stood on the doorstep. As yet unaware of what was happening inside, one of them smiled at Anica and asked,

"Excuse me miss. Are your parents home? We found a car registered to this address..."

The officer who had been speaking stopped when he saw the terror in her eyes. Anica finally found her words.

"My, my father, he's beating my brother and he won't stop. He's hurt! Please help him! Help my brother!"

"Where is this happening, miss?"

An angry shout from the kitchen gave him his answer.

"Who y'all talkin' to, you little whore? Yer aunt? Y'think that fat hog gonna do somethin'?"

The officers rushed toward the kitchen, with Anica close behind. John stood up, the lash still in his hand. One of the officers took a yellow gun from his belt and pointed it at her father. The other drew his 9mm automatic.

"Step away from the boy, " the one with the yellow gun commanded. "On the floor, face down, put your hands behind your head!"

John scowled defiantly at them.

"This here, this here's a family matter, ain't none o' yer business!"

"On the floor, face down, hands behind your head."

John stood his ground, tightening his grip on his belt. The officer with the yellow gun fired. A barbed projectile attached to two hair-thin coils of wire struck John in the chest. He jerked involuntarily for a moment, then fell with a thud onto the floor, writhing and twitching. The cop with the automatic stepped between him and Joshua, and together the officers held him down and handcuffed him behind his back. The officer who had tasered John put his knee in the small of John's back. Keeping his hand on the butt of his automatic, he commanded John not to move. He did not move.

The other cop knelt to attend to Joshua. Anica rushed in, crying hysterically. The officer told her she had to keep back, and raised an arm to keep her from approaching further. Anica stopped but did not retreat.

"Josh! Josh!" she cried. Joshua was able to raise his head and he tried to smile when his eyes met hers.

"Don't try to move, son." Joshua did not, but he kept his eyes on his sister.

The sound of sirens wailed outside, growing louder, then stopped. Two paramedics entered, unfolding a gurney. Two more policemen followed. The four officers picked John up from the floor. Noticing the streaming wound in his calf, one of the paramedics told the cops, "Hey, we're going to have to look at that."

The cop who had tasered John addressed him curtly. "Not you. Tend to the boy. "

They dragged John through the front door and shoved him into the back of a police car. The officers who had arrived with the paramedics took him away, while the other two returned to the house. They moved the kitchen table out of the way while the paramedics worked on Joshua. One of them placed her hand on his back, where John had stomped him to the floor.

"We've got some internal bleeding here. We need to move, stat!"

The paramedics carefully rolled Joshua onto a hardwood stretcher, snugged some straps, and placed him carefully, but quickly, onto the gurney. As they began to roll it towards the door, Anica ran after them.

"I'm coming with you! I'm coming. That's my brother!"

Aunt Alice filled up the front door. The paramedics ordered her sharply to move aside.

"What's happened here? What happened to my nephew?" she cried.

The paramedics ignored her and rolled Joshua toward the waiting ambulance. The officer who had first spoken to Anica held her arms, gently but firmly, as she tried to run after them. As the ambulance door closed, she fell to her knees.

"Joshua!" she screamed.

Aunt Alice rushed to Anica as quickly as she could. She tried to gather her into her arms, but she stayed on her knees, arms tightly crossed in front of her.

"I need to be with my brother!" she shouted defiantly to the officer who had restrained her.

Aunt Alice asked him, "Where are they taking him?"

"Glen Park Medical Center," he answered.

"My God, his mother is there. Let me take my niece."

The officer knelt before Anica and put his hands on her shoulders. "How would you like a ride in a police car?" he asked her.

Understanding what he was telling her, Anica quickly nodded. The officer escorted her out of the door and opened the back door of his cruiser for her.

The other officer turned to Aunt Alice as he followed. "We'll be sirens and lights, ma'am." One of us will wait with her outside the emergency room."

Joshua was barely conscious, still strapped to the uncomfortable board, as he was wheeled into the emergency entrance. The paramedics spoke to the waiting nurses.

"Miller. Joshua Miller. His aunt says his mother is in IC here. She'll be along in a few minutes. Alice Adler. Big woman, you can't miss her."

They undid the restraints and helped to slide Joshua

off the board onto another gurney. The overhead lights blurrily moved by above him until he was brought into a room. A nurse attached a blood pressure cuff to his good arm and placed a clip with a red light on his fingertip. Another pair of nurses got to work with scissors, quickly cutting away his clothes. Joshua felt embarrassed and cold, but he was too weak to protest. One of them finally pulled a thin blanket over his legs and midsection.

A doctor entered and shone a penlight into his eyes. He moved the light from side to side and asked Joshua to follow it with his eyes. Seeming satisfied, he motioned to a nurse who was waiting nearby with a hypodermic. She pulled the blanket down and stabbed him in the thigh with it, compounding his indignity. A few moments later, though, he felt something warm and soothing coursing through him, and the pain he seemed to have everywhere receded. The doctor with the penlight reached under him to feel the swelling on his back.

"Joshua? We're going to take some pictures, and then we're going to take you upstairs and give you something that will make you sleep."

"You mean I'm going to have surgery, don't you?" Joshua asked him scornfully.

A nurse entered and told the doctor there was a policeman outside with a little girl in a bathrobe. She says she's his sister and she has to see him, the nurse explained.

"Ani!" Joshua shouted as loudly as he could. It made the injury to his ribs hurt, but he shouted again. "Ani!"

"Josh!" his sister's voice called to him from nearby. The doctor nodded to the nurse, and a moment later, his sister and one of the policemen who had rescued him entered the room. Anica ran to his bedside. The doctor told her she couldn't get any closer and she could only have a couple of minutes. Joshua defiantly flicked the glowing clip off his finger and held out his hand. Anica took it and no one stopped her. She bit a knuckle on her other hand and sobbed. Joshua squeezed her hand more tightly.

"Ani. Ani, I need you to be strong right now. They're going to do a bunch of stuff to me, and you're going to make sure they do it right. You'll get to see me later."

To the doctor, pointedly, "Won't she!"

"It's your turn to watch over me, okay? Promise?"

"Promise," she told him through her tears.

Some people in gray scrubs came into the room to take Joshua for X-rays. As they wheeled him out, Joshua repeated,

"Promise!"

"Promise." She answered him.

The late afternoon sunlight shone into Joshua's

room. He was propped up in bed, but it was difficult for him to move very much. There was a cast on his right forearm and his shoulder was bound with what seemed to be a hundred Ace bandages. There was an IV stuck into the back of his good hand, which annoyed Joshua to no end. The left side of his back was heavily bandaged and his ribs were taped up. He'd been denied even the paltry dignity of a hospital gown, but there were blankets covering his legs and midsection.

Anica sat in a chair by the edge of his bed. She offered him a cup with a straw in it. He took a couple of sips and frowned.

"Ginger ale. Don't they have anything else in this place to drink but ginger ale?"

"I think they have Sprite," Anica told him.

"I hate Sprite." Joshua muttered. "And I'm hungry! I want a cheeseburger! French fries! I want a chocolate milkshake!"

"Restricted diet for you, young man! At least for a while. If I can do it, you can do it!" his mother's voice called out gently.

Mom sat in a wheelchair on the other side of the bed from Anica. A nurse's aide stood patiently behind her. Agnes turned to address her.

"I need a few minutes with my children, if you don't mind."

"I'm supposed to stay with you," the aide told her.

278

"A few minutes!" she snarled. The aide turned to leave, saying she would wait right outside.

"I don't know why they're still rolling me around me in this thing," Agnes said. "I feel fine."

"Speak for yourself, Mom," Joshua admonished her. He'd been in intensive care for two days after his surgery. Joshua had a ruptured kidney that they were able to save, in addition to a badly dislocated shoulder, four broken ribs, and a fracture to his right ulna. The other injuries his father had inflicted were superficial, but they still hurt.

"Mom, what did they do with - God, I hate him, Mom. I hope they never let him out!"

"Joshua, your f – John was a good man once. Maybe there's still some good inside of him. He's sick, very sick in his head, but it doesn't excuse what he did. He will be going away for quite a while, and he will never live with us or near us again. I'm divorcing him of course. I told him so before – well, maybe that's what finally made him snap.

"What happened to him?"

"Joshua, his father – it took him a long time before he would talk to me about it. It happens a lot that when children are hurt by their parents, they grow up to hurt their own children. He tried to provide for you, but he could never let himself be close to either of you. Maybe because – well, when people are stressed, it can bring out the worst in them. His business was failing.

He'd worked so hard to build it up, coming up from nothing. And he had problems with women. When I thought he might hurt Ani, I had to put a stop to it. I made him sleep downstairs and told him to stay away from both of you. He told me he was looking for an apartment. I was going to throw him out regardless when I had this damn thing happen."

Agnes started to cry. "I'm so, so sorry, Josh. Ani, I'm so, so sorry! Why didn't I see it sooner?" Anica crossed to the other side of the bed to embrace her mother. Joshua couldn't move, but he turned his head and told her,

"It's all right, Mom. We're going to be okay, and we have each other."

Agnes composed herself and blew her nose with the tissues Joshua couldn't reach. The aide returned to take her back to her room.

"So grown up! You're so grown up now, and so brave. Joshua, I am so proud of you. So proud of you."

Anica returned to his side after their mother left. She offered him the cup and the straw again, but Joshua made a face at her.

"Well ... I can't get you a cheeseburger, but maybe I can smuggle in some root beer. You like root beer."

Joshua smiled at his sister. She was growing up, more beautiful every day. And she was happy, in spite of everything that had happened. And safe. She was safe.

A beam of sunlight reflected crazily from something newly in the room. Joshua turned his head towards the door. Becky Lindstrom stood just inside, holding the string of a big Mylar balloon. Under her arm she had an enormous red envelope. When Joshua's eyes met hers, she said,

"You stood me up!"

Joshua laughed. "I was a little busy," he told her. Becky clipped the string of the balloon to the foot of his bed. She opened the big red envelope to reveal the biggest greeting card he'd ever seen. It said "Get Well Soon!" and it was covered with notes and signatures. Becky opened it up, and there were more of them. A lot more.

"I got all of them," Becky said proudly. "The whole school! Everyone! And all of your teachers, and even the cafeteria ladies. You're a celebrity now, Joshua Miller!" Becky turned to Anica, who had been smiling silently. "Oh my God, where are my manners?" Becky extended her hand. "You must be Ani! Joshua doesn't talk about anything but you. Joshua, are you going to introduce us?"

"Um, Ani, this is my friend Becky. Becky Lindstrom. Becky, this is my sister, Anica."

Anica graciously shook Becky's hand, then turned to Joshua. In a stage whisper, she said,

"Becky Lindstrom? *The* Becky Lindstrom?"

Joshua's face reddened. Addressing Becky, Anica

281

said, "That's funny. Since he woke up, all he talks about is you."

Joshua's face reddened even more. Anica rose to leave. Smiling mischievously, she said, "I'm going to go see Mom. I'll leave you and your *friend* alone for a while."

Becky approached and occupied the chair Anica had been using, scooting it closer to his bed. She wore faded denim short shorts with sequins on them and a light blue top with spaghetti straps that she could *not* have worn to school. On her feet were a pair of fancy open-toed sandals. Her toenails were painted in the same sparkly blue as her fingernails. In her ears, she wore the little topaz earrings that sparkled in the light, like the rest of her.

She sparkles, Joshua thought, *all over, all of her, that's what she does. She sparkles.*

The End

Afterword

When I started this book, I had intended to write a few connected short stories poking some fun at works like Jeff Kinney's *Diary Of A Wimpy Kid* and James Patterson's *Middle School* series. I read these excellent books with my daughter a few years ago, and it occurred to me that they would make good fodder for satire. I thought I might post them for my relatively few Facebook friends and Twitter followers in hopes of getting a laugh or two.

Most of the major characters in *Joshua* were born of this endeavor, but as I began writing about them, they soon took me in a different direction. The stories took on a more serious tone, and after I'd penned a few of them, I started to stitch them together, adding and changing material as needed to make the story fluid and to bring it to a meaningful conclusion.

The result was the first draft of this book. It was only a bit over seventy pages pages long in the font and format I was working with – far too long for a short story. I did not know what to do with it, but I was too far in to abandon the project.

Although by then I had most of the plot elements firmly in place, my characters clearly had much more to tell me about themselves. It was also clear by then that almost all of the satirical elements I'd originally intended no longer belonged in this story. In fact,

Joshua had become something rather dark.

As I set about rewriting most of the first half of the story and struggled to give meaningful depth to my characters, it soon became clear I was writing a novel, even though this was not what I'd started out to do. Had I intended this at the outset, I don't know if I could have started it.

Joshua is my first foray into fiction in the thirty years that have passed since I wrote the satirical *Spike Bike* stories, for which I am still somewhat known[*]. I am nearly seventy now. At various times in my life, I have believed that I might have a novel in me, but I would never have believed it would be a story like this one.

I started writing stories when I was a child, always with the intent of getting a laugh from my readers, however few they might be. I had some success with this, or some fun at least, even though I never thought of myself as a writer – certainly not as a serious one. The unexpected success of *Spike Bike* gave me pause to think otherwise, but the increasing demands of my career – i.e., my day job – and my quest to build a life for myself put my writing ambitions on hold.

---

[*]You can find these on the Internet with any search engine. In 1989, I sold a couple of them to a magazine named *Cyclist*, but it went out of business not long after.

Now that my life is largely over and my career most certainly is, I've found that I still have some stories to tell. While I have hardly lost my sense of humor, I seem to have found a capacity to break away from what I did in the past.

One thing has not changed. Any story begins with one or more characters and a setting in which to place them. I might have an idea at the outset of how the story will come out, but it's been my experience in every instance that the characters take on a life of their own, living their stories while I just write them down as they unfold.

There is, of course, nothing mystical in this process. Everything that comes out of a writer's head had to have been there to begin with. The act of story writing evokes memories and feelings that are often long-buried. The process can be cathartic, and even painful at times, but this is what brings the characters to life.

Although *Joshua* is unequivocally a work of fiction, the people, places, situations, and events I created are all impressions of people, places, situations, and events that I have encountered in my lifetime. As that lifetime has been long, perhaps a novel is the only thing this story could ever have been.

Robert Fishell
Naperville, Illinois, February 2019
www.bobfishell.com

About the Author

Robert Fishell is the author of the short story series *The Adventures Of Spike Bike,* which were first serialized on the Internet in 1988 and 1989 and published in the magazine *Cyclist.*

He is a native of Ohio, where he lived until 1977. He now lives in Illinois with his wife and daughter.

He has degrees in Electrical Engineering, Computer Science, and Secondary Education, along with decades of hard knocks that have proved to be far more instructional than his formal education.

After a career spanning 37 years, he retired in 2014 and now devotes most of his time to his family.

In addition to writing, he enjoys road and mountain biking, playing keyboard instruments, singing (when no one can hear him), and tinkering with mechanical things.

Although he has been writing stories since childhood, *Joshua* is his first publication since 1989, and his first novel.

Made in the USA
Columbia, SC
17 December 2019